Books by Colin Neenan

IDIOT!

IN YOUR DREAMS

LIVE A LITTLE

A love story with drama,
betrayal and e-mail

Colin Neenan

Brown Barn Books
Weston, Connecticut

Brown Barn Books,
a division of Pictures of Record, Inc.
119 Kettle Creek Road, Weston, Connecticut 06883, U.S.A.
www.brownbarnbooks.com

IDIOT!
Copyright © 2004 by Colin Neenan
Original paperback edition

The characters and events to be found in these pages are fictitious. Any resemblance to actual persons living or dead is purely coincidental.

Library of Congress Control Number: 2004101789
ISBN: 0-9746481-1-6
Neenan, Colin
IDIOT!

Printed in the United States of America

To Alix and Cadence

One

I don't expect you to believe this, but I'm not a complete idiot.

I realize it doesn't look good. When you become famous because you do something stupid and someone comes along and takes this unbelievable photograph of you doing it, the world is bound to think you're a moron. And it's not going to help when your girlfriend writes a best-seller telling exactly how you ended up doing that stupid thing. Add to that how I've stuttered through half the talk-shows we've been on, and add to that how the magazines quote only the dumbest things I say, and I'm lucky people don't take one look at me and burst out laughing.

Of course, it's not going to help my reputation, buying six bags of groceries and locking myself in a hotel room three thousand miles from home in San Diego, California. Not that I'm torturing myself. I'm on the twenty-second floor, have this beautiful view of the ocean with sparkles reflecting off the water, have a clean bathroom and a microwave and a little refrigerator and a computer and Internet access and a week's worth of my favorite food—pretty good for a seventeen-year-old kid—but still, it never makes a guy look good, locking himself in a hotel room and threatening to blow his head off if anyone touches the door.

Just for the record, I don't have a gun. I've got a black water pistol that might look like a real gun from six blocks away, but my mom's a foaming-at-the-mouth gun-control person, and the idea of actually having a gun anywhere in this room would completely freak me out.

I hope Mom and Dad know this. I know they're going to have heart attacks when the police tell them what's going on, and I know they're probably already on a plane out here, but I really hope they know I'm bluffing. I'm hoping they talk to Zanny and Mr. Nelson and Dr. Hackinfire and they all convince each other I'm bluffing, but I'm also hoping they're not able to convince anybody else. I mean, Zanny, especially, knows I'm not crazy, but I'm banking on the police not taking her word for it. If they do, I'm screwed. If they break down the door, all I can do is hold this water pistol up to my head and look like a complete idiot.

So what else is new?

At this point I'm going to look like a complete idiot no matter what. Either for locking myself in here or for the talk-shows and interviews I've been doing for the last month and a half, take your pick. It'll probably depend on how crazy Mr. Nelson makes me look. Because that's what he's going to do; he's probably already working on it, already leaking to the press a whole list of crazy things I've done. He's not about to just sit back and let me tell America they've been tricked, they've been lied to. For weeks he'd been bugging me to finish writing my book, finish writing the companion book to Zanny's *Love Doesn't Grow on Trees,* but that all changed in Minneapolis. Back when Zanny and I were in Minneapolis, Mr. Nelson decided I couldn't be trusted to write a book, couldn't be trusted to stay on message, and he started doing everything he could to stop me from writing the book.

Which is why I've locked myself in here. I figure it's the only way I'll get a chance to write this thing, the only way I'll get a chance to talk about what really happened. If I hadn't locked myself in here, if I'd just told Mr. Nelson I was going to take some time off and finish writing the book, I have a feeling he would have had me carted off to Saint Uwell's. He actually mentioned Saint Uwell's to me back in Minneapolis, called it a resort where I could go and rest for a while, if I wanted. Even on the Internet it looks like this great vacation place. It wasn't until I found a website written by a seventeen-year-old (my age) ex-patient that I discovered it's really a loony bin.

It's not that I'm ungrateful. I appreciate everything Mr. Nelson has done for me and Zanny, I swear to God. We've already made more money than most teachers make in a lifetime. We have book deals, a movie deal, a television deal, even a greeting card deal. Everywhere we go people tell us how good-looking we are. I always thought I was

OK-looking, but now girls are watching me, they're smiling at me. People want to shake our hands, they want to be near us, they want to touch us, they want to feed us. One guy in Akron wanted to smell us.

And, as Zanny points out every day, it's great. I never thought much about ever being famous, but the truth is, being famous is really fun. Somehow, Zanny knew that since she was three. Zanny was determined to be famous. First by ice-skating, then by saving animals, then by card tricks, then by writing novels, and then, since eighth grade, by being an investigative reporter. For three years she's been carrying a notebook, nosing around, looking for the right story, the perfect story. She's been convinced that all she's needed to become famous is the right story—a story that would instantly capture the imagination of the American public.

Little did I know that on a cold Monday night in February, I was going to help her find it. Little did I know that I was going to do one stupid thing and some random photographer was going to take this amazing picture of me doing this thing, and I was going to become rich and famous by looking like a total idiot.

Which I'm not. Seriously. I'm not the nice dumb guy Zanny makes me look like in *Love Doesn't Grow on Trees*. I'm not that dumb, and I'm not that nice. The problem is, Zanny explains stuff, but she only explains certain stuff.

The play, for instance. In *Love Doesn't Grow on Trees*, Zanny says:

> *The four of us decided to audition for the play.*

That's it. The four of us decided to audition for the play.

Well. . . yeah. Technically, that's correct, but she makes it sound like the four of us just spontaneously decided to try out for the play, just for the hell of it. Which makes me sound like a. . . theater person. I'm not a theater person. I don't try to make everything sound like the end of the world. I don't do mime.

No, I tried out for the play because Gene was obsessed with Tufts University. That's why I tried out.

We were in the back of the Brew Ha Ha and Zanny was using the wooden stirrer to scoop latte foam out of the bottom of her cup. Casually, like he was talking about the weather, Gene mentioned he was going to audition for *A Midsummer Night's Dream*.

"What," I said, staring at him. "You're going to hang out with Bertram Diller?" Last winter, Bertram Diller actually started wearing a cape to school.

"Look," Gene explained, calmly. "Tufts is *most* competitive. I need something."

"What are you talking about? You've got lots of somethings."

"Arts editor of the newspaper? You don't think Tufts is going to see right through arts editor?"

"So what? Didn't you start that save-the-world club?"

"We don't do anything," Gene whined. "Nobody sees the point."

"What about the car wash?"

"Do you know how many cars we washed? Seven. Seven little cars."

"What. You were expecting to actually change the world?" I threw my hands up. "You think Tufts counted how many cars you washed?"

Gene was obsessed with college. Or more specifically, with Tufts University. Gene's great-grandfather had gone there, and his grandfather had gone there, and his dad was supposed to go there but was too into being a drugged-out rock star to bother with college. Ten years ago, when his dad left his mom for a yoga instructor with big boobs, it became Gene's life dream to go to Tufts and show up his dad.

So it wasn't much of a surprise when Gene waved his hand at me like he was already feeling the espresso jitters. "I'm trying out, so leave me alone."

"And I think it's great!" Mary cheered, hugging his arm. Pressing his arm against the side of her breast, I noticed. They'd been going out for over a year now. Zanny claimed they still weren't doing it, but I had a feeling she was wrong.

"It is great," Zanny agreed. "It takes courage to try something new like that."

"Especially when it's Shakespeare!" Mary added, patting Gene on the knee and then leaving her hand there. God, talk about depressing. In the eighth grade, if someone had told me Gene Fusco would lose his virginity before I did, I might have had to shoot myself. Not that Gene was ugly or anything. He was tall, dark, and maybe even handsome, I don't know. But he was Gene. He couldn't dribble a basketball, he stacked his books largest to smallest. The first time he met Mary was in the library.

"Hey, you know what?" Zanny said, waving her hand, palm up.

Oh, shit. It was bad news, Zanny waving her hand, palm up. The last time she'd waved her hand, palm up, we'd sprinkled sneezing powder in Mr. Wilson's desk and sent him to the hospital with a non-stop nosebleed. I looked over at Zanny, saw her pull a hand through her shiny black hair, saw it fall right back into her face.

"You know what?" she repeated, leaning forward. "I think we should all try out."

"Yeah. Right."

"I'm serious!" she said, elbowing me.

Like I didn't know she was serious. Like I wasn't desperate to turn this around. "I'm going to try out for Shakespeare?" I asked. "It'd be like doing a play in freaking French."

"I think it could be cool," Zanny said.

"Cool?"

"Why not?" Mary agreed, sounding like the agreeable side-kick on a talk-show.

"Let's do it." Zanny started clapping her hands together fast like the football team does when they're pumping themselves up to rip the heads off the other team. "Do it. Do it. Do it. Do it. Do it."

"Do it. Do it. Do it," Mary joined in, clapping with her.

"OK, can everyone calm down a second?" I asked, trying to think of a way out of this.

"Oh, James," Zanny said, grabbing my arm like Mary had just grabbed Gene's, only without pressing it against the side of her breast. "You need to learn how to live."

I pulled my arm back. I hated it when she called me James. James meant I was too stuffy, too wimpy, too scared. James meant I didn't know how to live.

James meant wuss.

And what was the big deal? It wasn't like she was trying to get me to jump out a window or do drugs or blow up the A-wing bathroom. She wanted me to try out for a play. How bad could it be?

Pretty bad, I told myself, as Zanny and I walked in through a door at the back of the auditorium. The entire place was dark except for a bright light shining down on center stage. I stopped in my tracks. Zanny stopped, too, and looked over her shoulder and pointed to the back row of seats.

"You don't need to audition," she said. "You can just sit back here in the dark and jerk off."

"Zanny—"

She didn't mention jerking off because it happened to be something we talked about. She mentioned it because it was something we never talked about, it was a weapon she used against me, something she knew would bug me. I'd made the mistake in ninth grade of refusing to admit to her that I had ever in my life jerked off. After that, whenever she wanted to get under my skin, she'd just say the word.

"I really think it's important you learn how to do it."

I held my palms up. "I'll see you later," I said, turning back.

"No, no, no, no, no," Zanny said, laughing, grabbing my arm. "I'll be good, I promise. I promise."

"I don't even know how to spell Shakespeare."

Zanny held on to my arm, pulling me slowly toward the front of the auditorium. "We're supporting Gene, remember?"

"Because he's dumb enough to try out for the play?"

"We're showing solidarity."

"This isn't a political movement."

Forty or fifty kids were hanging out down at the front of the auditorium. Gene was over by the stairs to the stage, yukking it up with George Hanson, a theater regular wearing the standard theater black t-shirt. The place was packed with theater regulars. Roger Jeevers. Lucy Thompson. Kevin M. Bacon, who used his middle initial so as not to be confused with the movie star. (Always a problem.) And there, right down below center stage was Bertram Diller, wearing his flowing black cape and dancing, waltzing, with Jennifer Franklin. It was astounding to me that someone who looked like Jennifer Franklin would acknowledge the existence of a Bertram Diller, but that was the way it worked with theater people. They come from a different planet.

"PEOPLE!" Mr. Fricker shouted, his voice erupting in the darkness, demanding silence. I had him for freshman English and thought he was a pompous jerk, but the guy knew how to shut people up. Zanny and I took seats in the third row.

Mr. Fricker walked down to the foot of the stage and turned and slowly looked at each and every one of us. "Are we ready?" he asked.

No. I wasn't ready. I hadn't even looked at the stupid play and had no idea what it was about other than the fact that some people were in love and therefore acting like idiots as they ran around speaking in iambic pentameter.

"The course of true love never did run smooth."

Zanny had quoted that line to me, had said it was from the play. Great. The thing was full of clichés.

"MINDY WILSON!" Mr. Fricker called, looking at his clipboard. "And FRANK STRICKLAND."

A small dagger went through my heart as I watched Mindy and Frank jump up on the stage and walk into the center stage spotlight and stand there holding these little books. I was going to be there. I'd signed up for the audition, and now I was going to have to stand up there and make a fool out of myself.

"I can't believe you made it." It was Gene, leaning forward in the seat behind me.

"Neither can I," I told him.

"SILENCE!" Mr. Fricker screamed, throwing a hand up in the air.

Zanny hit my chest with the back of her hand. I sat and crossed my arms, my heart jack-hammering each time two people stopped reading and Mr. Fricker looked at his clipboard. I was worn out by the time he got to us.

"ZANNY MANNING," he said, finally. "And JIM O'REILLY."

I still could have bolted. Could have walked away. Instead I climbed up onstage and grabbed one of the little books.

"We start right there," Zanny said, pointing to a spot in my book where someone had written in thick black letters, BEGIN HERE.

"OK," I told her, swallowing as Zanny read a line. She rattled it off in no time, and for a second I didn't know it was my line. Eventually, just as I realized it, Zanny was reaching over, trying to point it out to me.

"OK, OK," I said. And started reading:

Oh, Helen, goddess, Nymph, perfect, divine!
To what, my love, shall I compare my eyne?
Crystal is muddy. Oh, how ripe in show
The lips, those kissing cherries—

"Stop, stop, stop, stop, STOP," Mr. Fricker called, walking down the center aisle through the dark of the auditorium. "Look—." He glanced down at his clipboard, then looked up at me. "Jim. Let me ask you. Have you ever been in love?"

I was standing at the edge of the stage, Mr. Fricker down below. I could have easily swung my leg and kicked him in the face.

"Have you ever been in love?"

I was nervous as hell, as it was, standing there center stage, under the only lights in the entire auditorium, saying these words I didn't understand, having a hard time even reading them because my right hand holding the little book was shaking. Why was he doing this?

Mr. Fricker looked back at his clipboard. "Have you ever been in love, Jim?" he asked, in his contemptuous hyper mode. He'd gone insane like this in class, too, whenever someone read a famous poem out loud and stumbled over words and completely butchered it. It was like Fricker took it personally.

"Have you?" he asked, when I didn't answer right away. "Have you ever been in love?"

What the hell was I supposed to say? No? Was I supposed to say no? Was it so obvious? The entire auditorium was completely quiet. Fifty or so kids sitting out in the auditorium, all of them watching me hanging there in the wind. Jodi Woodrow. Lisa Kellerman. Bart Fulton. Exchanging looks, smiles. They loved Mr. Fricker. Loved how he could do this to people.

"It's a simple yes or no question," he said, his hands bubbling up in the air like he was re-enacting a volcano. "Have you ever been in love? Have you ever connected to one person in a way that was completely different from how you felt about anyone else in the entire world?"

I don't know why, but my eyes suddenly glanced at Zanny, and my heart flopped like a fish in the bottom of a row boat.

"Yes," I whispered, looking away quickly.

"Yes?" Mr. Fricker asked, incredulous.

And I looked at him dead on, only realizing it that very second. "Yes."

"You've been in love?" he asked.

I couldn't look at him, couldn't look at Zanny. Just looked off into the blackness of the auditorium, feeling it in my heart. An alive, ripping feeling in my heart. "Yes," I said.

"Then SOUND like it!" Mr. Fricker shouted, the only person I'd ever met who spoke in capital letters. "Sound in LOVE. Do you remember? Do you remember loving someone passionately and not being able to tell her? Not being able to say a word? And now suddenly HERE'S YOUR CHANCE! You can talk to her, you can say what you feel for the first time EVER. This is it. This is your chance. You will never have another opportunity EVER to say these things. SAY THEM!"

No one moved. I got goose bumps.

This was it. This was my chance.

Two

I was in love. Completely, absolutely in love. Asthma-attack, desperate-to-catch-your-breath in love.

I'm embarrassed saying how in love I was because apparently it's not at all a guy thing. It's been something that's come up a lot on the talk-shows, this in love thing. Guys, apparently, do not panic like I did, do not obsess about being in love. It's OK to obsess about someone dumping you. In *Love Doesn't Grow On Trees,* Zanny talks about how Gene flips out when Mary dumps him, and we haven't met anyone who thinks that's weird. Getting dumped you can be wacked about if you're a guy, but not being in love. Apparently it's OK for a guy to love a girl, just as long as there's none of this not knowing what to do, none of this not being able to look at her, none of this adrenaline sprayed on an open heart. They'd shown us a movie in middle school of this dissected frog, the whole rib cage opened up, the heart, the guts exposed. And then they sprayed some adrenaline on the thing, and suddenly the heart was beating like mad, like the poor guy was terrified and desperate to get away.

I wasn't terrified, but I sure as hell wanted to get away. And apparently a lot of people think that's cute. It's like the photograph in the papers, the world-famous photograph that started this whole thing in the first place. Everyone talks about how cute I look, staring down with that deer-in-the-headlights look in my eyes. I cringe when a reporter or a talk-show host starts talking about the freaking photograph. Cute. How cute. You're so cute! One woman in a studio audience in Santa Monica used the word adorable. Give me a sledgehammer and show me her car. I'll show her adorable.

I have no memory of reading the lines over again. On page nine of *Love Doesn't Grow on Trees,* Zanny talks about this different voice coming out of me the second time we read the lines, as if some Shakespearean actor had decided to inhabit my body. She made it sound just like the exorcism Grandma claimed she'd witnessed when she was six, only Zanny said nothing about my head spinning around.

All I know is we read the lines again and I put the book down on the stage and started walking. I needed to get away from Zanny, and I headed straight for the stairs leading off the stage. I couldn't see a thing in the darkness, after being under the spotlight like that, and I was afraid I was going to walk straight off the stage, but it didn't slow me down.

"Jimmy," Zanny called after me. "Jim."

I leapt down the steps. Zanny caught up with me halfway to the back of the auditorium.

"Where do you think you're going?"

"Home," I told her.

"Are you kidding me? You can't go home."

"Watch."

"Why? Because you didn't like the way Fricker treated you?"

"Sure," I said. If that was what Zanny thought, at least it wouldn't involve any explaining.

"But you did it! You did exactly what he said. You were incredible! He's definitely going to want to hear you read again."

I headed straight for the lighted red exit sign in the back of the auditorium.

"Don't you understand?" Zanny went on. "He decides parts today. That's the way Fricker does it. He sorts out all the parts today."

"Then I'm not getting one," I said, moving faster, ready to run if I had to.

"Of course you're getting one! That's what I'm trying to tell you." Zanny grabbed my arm. We'd been friends since we were three, she'd grabbed my arm lots of times, but this was the first time her fingers felt like they scorched my skin. This was the first time she was pretty, beautiful, green eyes, black hair, pale Irish skin.

"Jimmy, you were unbelievable," she said. "I'm completely serious. I stood up there, reading those lines with you, and I felt like you loved me. You read them just like Mr. Fricker said. Like you were really in love with me."

"I'll see you tomorrow."

"But Jimmy—"

"QUIET!" Mr. Fricker called, his voice echoing through the auditorium. I turned and shoved open the door into the bright fluorescents of the hallway, breathing like I'd been deep underwater and had just broken the surface.

Outside rain was really coming down. I ran to my car, jumped in and slammed the door hard.

Don't you understand? she'd asked me. Don't you understand?

I understood, all right. I understood that I couldn't look at her, couldn't listen to her, couldn't be around her. I understood that I was drowning here, and that what I should really do is drop out of school and move away. That was the safest thing, the smartest thing. Get away and don't come back. Although now that I was away from her, now that I was alone in the car, rain washing down the windshield, I was fine. Better than fine. I was in love. With Zanny. I didn't get how it happened, didn't get why today. Did she have a new haircut? A different perfume? There was only one thing I knew for sure.

I was in love with Zanny. I was in love with Suzannah Ursula Manning. Zanny.

I bit my lip, trying to think of what to do. I wanted to talk to someone, tell someone, but who? Gene? Had Gene felt like this about Mary? It was possible, I supposed, but if he did, he'd done a hell of a job hiding it. But if not Gene, then who? Who did I know who would understand? Who was out there who'd felt like this?

Besides Dad.

Dad, I knew, had felt like this. I knew this because when my sister Robin drove home from college after junior year ready to overthrow the government, Mom and Dad took us all to this fancy seafood restaurant. Dad had two martinis talking to Robin about politics, and Mom had almost a whole bottle of wine because Robin was really getting on her nerves. Dad snuck another martini when Mom wasn't looking, and suddenly he had us three kids huddled together—me and my twin brother Jake and Robin—and he told us about Mom back in college and how he'd loved her so much she took his breath away. He told us how one night he couldn't get to sleep, thinking about her, and how he'd climbed out his window and sat on the ledge in the cold spring night, wrapped in a blanket, watching the sunrise, thinking about her, and then how he went to her room and knocked and invited her to breakfast and asked her to marry him.

So Dad had felt this, this live-animal-inside feeling.

Not that I was ever going to try to talk to him about it, not that this was something I would even mention to Dad. But still, it was nice knowing someone else could be this stupid.

I started the car and turned on the wipers. As they swiped the rivulets off the windshield, I saw a car parked in the faculty row with its wipers going. It was a little red sports car, facing my direction, behind the wheel was Ms. Farling, my English teacher. Ms. Farling, the best teacher in the school, acting out scenes in books, playing her keyboard, grabbing people out of their seats to dance with them. She was hyper, always moving, so it was weird to see her just sitting there in her car.

I leaned forward and squinted. Was she crying? At first I thought it was just the rain, but then I saw her wipe her eyes with the back of her wrist. She was crying. Ms. Farling just didn't seem like the crying kind, and it seemed like I should do something.

But as I was sitting there trying to think, Ms. Farling noticed my windshield wipers and stared at me and seemed horrified, her body lurching, like someone had stuck a knife in her side. She dropped her head, hiding her face with both hands like criminals do, leaving the courthouse. What the hell? I blinked a couple of times, looking at her, but then wanted to get away as fast as possible. I backed out without looking. What was wrong with Ms. Farling? Why was she so upset that I saw her? She wasn't stealing a car, she was crying. Why did she think it was so horrible that one of her students saw her cry?

It made no sense to me why she looked guilty.

I drove slowly through the parking lot and stopped at the light in front of school, almost hypnotized by the wipers swatting angrily at the streaming water. I didn't want the light to change. I wanted to just sit here in the car and watch the rain and worry about Ms. Farling and think about kissing Zanny. I knew how to kiss her. We'd talked about the people we'd kissed, and what we thought they did right and wrong. Zanny hated how guys didn't take their time with their tongues. Did they think it was a race? Some kind of contest? I knew I'd get it right, kissing Zanny. She'd love it. She'd—

Honk.

The light was green and the car behind me didn't feel like waiting. I took my foot off the brake and accelerated slowly, like I was worried about the car suddenly careening out of control. This was crazy. I went up Nottingham Hill and drove around the rich, woodsy part of town, where things stopped looking like the suburbs of New Jersey. You go up around the Hill and it's hard to believe you're forty miles from New York City. I just drove, enjoying the rain and the wind knocking the last of the leaves out of the trees and the craziness of being in love with Zanny Manning. This was insane. I knew Zanny. I knew she was not a good person to love. She was heartlessly honest. Impossible to pin down. Moody, flighty. Smart, funny, sexy.

I laughed out loud. Zanny would've laughed, too, that I was going around thinking of her as sexy.

When I got home, I parked in Dad's spot in the garage because he'd complain less than Mom about having to get wet. As soon as I got out of the car I could hear Jake's music thumping through the walls.

Jake.

My twin brother, Jake.

I'd completely forgotten about Jake. I hadn't forgotten he existed— I'd forgotten he was the single worst reason for falling in love with Zanny Manning.

I walked across the garage and up the two steps and through the door into the kitchen.

Knocking down the wall, just knocking down the wall.

The music was louder than my heart. Jake's room was on the second floor over at the other end of the house, but loud music was like a religion for him. I stood in the middle of kitchen and felt a cold helplessness filling my chest.

Zanny was crazy about him.

Absolutely insane. At the beach the summer before, she'd told me that Jake would make a great cult leader, that she'd join his cult if he started one.

"There's something different about him," Zanny said.

"Yeah, he doesn't cut his hair," I told her, grabbing a handful of sand and watching it slip out of my fist. Jake and I weren't identical, but when we were little, people said we looked almost exactly alike. The difference now was Jake was a little taller and I cut my hair and used a brush.

With the scruffy beard and the long hair, Jake reminded people of Jesus Christ. Zanny thought the Jesus thing was also due to Jake's charisma, but I thought it was mostly due to marijuana. Jake smoked a lot of pot, and that made him move slowly and smile a lot, which is how most people think Jesus would act.

Knock down the walls. Knocking down the walls. Knock knock knocking walls.

I was starving. I pulled open the fridge, looking for something, anything. Nobody bought food anymore. The only thing left in the refrigerator were condiments, including three different types of mustard, Dad's vitamins, and carrots. No pickles, even. Did Jake take the whole jar up to his room? Was he hoarding pickles?

I made myself a peanut butter and honey sandwich and leaned against the counter. When we were little I used to dream about the police coming and taking Jake away. Jake would break a toy or hit me or mush sand in my face, and Mom would say that was wrong, very, very wrong, and I would imagine the police getting wind of what was going on and showing up to cart him off. Didn't people get arrested for doing things that were very wrong? Couldn't they come and take Jake away? For a couple of weeks at least? Or maybe forever?

I stuffed what was left of the sandwich in my mouth and got out my math book and immediately thought of checking e-mail. It was my routine every day, to get my math homework done. As soon as I finished math, I could check e-mail. Then I had to get the rest of my homework done before I could check again or instant message or talk on the telephone.

Now I didn't want to wait. Math didn't matter. I just wanted to see if I had any messages from Zanny.

She was the main reason I checked e-mail in the first place. It was another way for us to talk, a way to say things we probably wouldn't say in person. At least I wouldn't say in person. Family stuff, sex stuff, meaning of life stuff. Most of the real things we talked about started with e-mail.

I sat down and opened my math book. Found the homework page but just stared at it, not even picking up my pencil. Real things. Zanny was the only person I talked to about real stuff. Zanny was the only person I'd ever met who wanted to talk about real stuff.

I looked over at the doorway to the family room, thinking about logging on. Had she e-mailed me from computer science? Zanny was so good at programming, she figured everything out in no time and spent half the period sending e-mail and checking stock prices. She usually sent me something, especially on Fridays, and now I was dying to check, to see if there was something, anything. We were going to the movies the next night with Gene and Mary. What did Zanny want to see? What did she say? What did she write to me? What words did she use? Was she funny? Was she serious? Suddenly everything she said was important. Everything she said, everything she thought, every breath she took. . . .

I grabbed my head with both hands, held my skull tightly between my outstretched fingers like it was a basketball someone was trying to knock out of my hands. So this was love. Wasn't that a song? Another song. I wished I could hear it, I wished I could hear again all the love songs I had ever heard. It felt like they would all speak to me, they would all have something to say, they would all tell me something about how I felt.

The phone rang.

I jumped. Jesus. Took a deep breath and waited for the second ring, but Jake must've picked up. Janine? Was he expecting a call from his girlfriend, Janine Johnson? I looked down at my textbook. The tangent of a 30-degree angle is zero. Which meant the cotangent is undefined. Nonexistent. Impossible.

I sat there and for the first time in my mathematical life thought about an undefined value. Thought about how mathematics could create a framework for something that did not exist. How could that be? How could they create something and then determine it does not exist?

Footsteps came thumping down the stairs. Jake. I grabbed my pencil and stuck my head in my book.

Jake slid into the kitchen and over to the refrigerator. He had the habit of never lifting his feet. Zanny said he looked like he was skating wherever he went.

"Dad said I should talk to you," Jake said, speaking into the refrigerator.

I waited. I was not an idiot, not with Jake. You never wanted to look anxious to hear what Jake had to tell you. If you sounded like you were dying to know, he'd never tell you. He'd just start talking in metaphors. It's sort of like this. It's kind of like that. Jake wrote poetry. He loved metaphors, loved not actually talking about what you were trying to talk about. Maybe that was why Zanny thought he sounded like a prophet, and why Grandma, before she died, still held out hope that he'd become a priest.

"About what?" I asked, not looking up from my book.

Instead of answering, Jake grabbed something out of the refrigerator and looked at me. I wrote down the wrong answer to number five just to look like I was doing something.

"*The Fall of Icarus*," Jake said, softly, smiling. I could hear him smiling, oh, God, here we go, he was going to start talking about something from ancient Greece. Or Latin. He was going to start reciting Latin. His poetry was full of that crap. People especially loved it when he translated Latin into druggie terms. *Carpe diem,* for instance, became smoke that doobie.

"Do you remember Mom showing us Breugel's *Fall of Icarus* at the museum?"

Art! Even worse! He was going to describe a painting Mom must have shown us ten years ago, back when she took us to museums. Back when she thought we would actually get something out of it.

"Icarus is in the background, golden-winged Icarus is plopping into the sea," Jake said, slowly, carefully, "as the peasants keep working in the fields, completely oblivious to what's going on."

Oh. Nice. I was a peasant. That was the point. Jake was calling me a peasant working in the fields, completely oblivious.

Did Jesus ever do this? Go around comparing other people to oblivious peasants working in the fields?

"It's your turn to set the table," I reminded him, still not looking up.

Jake laughed—a snot-filled snorting kind of sneeze. And Zanny was crazy about this guy! Thought he was brilliant. Profound. Charismatic.

Not what you want to hear about your twin brother. Especially coming from a girl you're in love with.

"Set the table," Jake said, like it was the punch line of a terrific joke. "Set the table."

I looked up. Jake was standing barefoot in a black t-shirt and jeans torn wide open in both knees. He was holding a beer can. He'd gotten a can of Miller's out of the refrigerator. Since when did he drink Dad's beer? They'd already taken away his driving privileges. What would they take away from him now?

He stood there, flat-footed, smiling at me.

"You need something?" I asked.

Jake's smile grew wide. "You have something to offer?"

I sat there. This always happened. If I'd had hours I might have thought of a decent comeback, but right there, right then, all I could do was look at the beer in his hand.

Which he opened with his middle finger. Standing there perfectly still, Jake opened the beer. Just opened the beer and still looking at me, drank down half the can.

"Mom's going to love that," I muttered, getting back to my book.

"Mom's gone," Jake said.

I wrote down the answer to the next problem. "What do you mean?" I asked, squinting at the book.

"I mean she ran away from home."

I stopped writing but forced myself not to look up. What the hell was he talking about? I knew Mom didn't run away, but I had a feeling she did something; something was going on. "Mom told you she's running away from home?"

From the corner of my eye, I saw Jake walk over and pull something off the front of the refrigerator. He walked back toward me and flicked a small square envelope onto my math book. On the front, in Mom's handwriting, was my name.

Jimmy

Shit. That was ominous. Jimmy. That was bad. Since the fourth grade Mom had stayed away from calling me Jimmy because she knew it drove me insane. It was OK other people calling me Jimmy, but for years Mom had sung me a song about Mommy and Jimmy, and by the fourth grade, Jimmy had to go. When Mom was really incredibly stressed, though, and crying or ready to cry or too hysterical to even cry, she'd forget how old I was and revert back to Jimmy.

For her to write *Jimmy* on the outside of an envelope was bad news.

"What is this?" I asked, moving my hands away from the envelope.

Jake finished his beer. "Dad says don't blame Mom, it's his fault."

I sat blinking at the freaking envelope. Mom had run away from home? From us? Just up and left? It didn't seem quite real. There must have been some misunderstanding.

"Want a beer?" Jake asked, opening up the refrigerator. Was Grandma up in heaven listening to this? Listening to her Father Jake over there?

"We have no idea where Mom's gone?" I asked.

"It's one of the requisite elements of running away, I think."

I sat there, shaking my head. This was unbelievable. Just completely unbelievable. This was Mom we were talking about. Who made sandwiches for lunch, who volunteered in the library back when we were in elementary school. So OK, so she joined that hippie group of women who lit candles and went around chanting. She was still Mom, though. Wasn't she?

"I bet they know," I said. "I bet the Circle Women know where she is."

Jake opened another beer. "Kind of scary. That's exactly what Dad said."

Just then the doorbell rang.

Mom. It was Mom. It had to be Mom. She couldn't just run away. Abandon us. She wouldn't do that.

Only why was she ringing the doorbell?

The police? Was it the police? State troopers? Were they bringing her back?

I held my breath as Jake sauntered out to the front door. Chain lock. Bolt lock. I swallowed.

"Where is good Demetrius?"

I jumped up. Gene. It was Gene.

"We need to talk to him."

And her. That was her. Zanny. She was out there, standing right out there.

I closed the math book on the note from Mom and made a run for it. I couldn't talk to Zanny right now, couldn't deal with her consoling me about Mom, couldn't deal with even seeing her.

I ran back to the family room, opened the sliding door, and slipped out into the mushy backyard, my heart pounding like someone was chasing me with a gun. I ran for the back fence and vaulted it, my legs swinging wildly and coming down on one of Mrs. McClintock's rose bushes. Damn. Thorns dug through my jeans as I climbed out of the bushes and crouched down below the fence, desperate to not let Zanny spot me.

Three

Of course if I'd had any idea back then that thousands of people would find it incredibly amusing that I jumped the fence, landing on Mrs. McClintock's clipped-back rose bushes, I probably would have just stayed there at the kitchen table with my math book. When you're not famous and you have no idea you're ever going to be famous, you don't go around wondering how things you do will look to people when you are famous.

In *Love Doesn't Grow on Trees*, Zanny doesn't even mention that my mom had just left. For weeks people thought it was just an ordinary Friday and I was this strange kid who didn't want to deal with this girl he was in love with and decided to sneak out of his house and jump a fence and land in some rose bushes.

No one ever mentioned that I'd just found out Mom had left. It wasn't until Seattle that someone seemed to get it. We were at the big bookstore downtown and Zanny was doing a reading from *Love Doesn't Grow on Trees*. Afterwards, the rose bushes came up, and the audience was having a good chuckle when a lady in a bright flowered dress stood up in tears.

"His mother had just run away from home!" she scolded them.

I wanted to kiss her, I wanted to give her money, I wanted to take her on the rest of the tour with us. I had no idea how she had found out, still have no idea how she found out that Mom had run away from home—a lot of websites and blogs had popped up about me and Zanny, so maybe the lady had found out about Mom through one of those. The point is, the lady was right. What was so funny? This kid's mom had just run away from home!

Zanny laughed at me at dinner up in the Space Needle that night. "Everyone knows it ends up OK in the end," she said. "It isn't like your mother jumped off a bridge or got shot by a Zulu warrior."

"It isn't like she ever comes back home, either," I pointed out.

I held my burger over my plate and watched Zanny as she nibbled her asparagus. "Look, Phil's right," Zanny said. She was talking about Phil Nelson, our manager. Phil Nelson, the famous agent from Holly-wood who had made us famous. Phil, Zanny called him. "People want the story," Zanny said. "If we give them the story, they'll come to see us, they'll buy our books (if you ever finish yours), they'll see our movie, they'll give us things. For free."

I sat there, just holding my burger. It was unbelievable the free stuff people were giving us. Barbeque sauce, sunglasses, diamond bracelets, Frisbees, bicycles, origami, pizza, cakes, pies, vacations, gold-plated paper clips, homemade noodles, pot, movie passes. In Des Moines, a waitress spilled spaghetti sauce on my shirt and a guy at the next table went out to his car and came back with one of his own shirts, which he and his wife insisted I keep. I would bet you could travel across the country for free, if you were famous enough. I would bet some movie stars could probably make money on the deal.

"But we have to stick to the story," Zanny went on. "It's a funny part of the story, when you jump the fence to get away from me and land in the rose bushes. America wants to laugh about it. People don't want to think about your mother."

I stared at Zanny. Stared because she was saying almost word for word what Phil Nelson had told me over the phone that morning. I almost asked her about it, almost came right out and asked Zanny point-blank if she and Mr. Nelson had been talking about this story business, had been colluding about sticking to the story. They sounded so much alike, what they said about it, I wondered if Mr. Nelson was calling Zanny when I wasn't around, coaching her about what to say and what not to say. Were the two of them talking about this stuff behind my back? Was Mr. Nelson trying to get Zanny to convince me that we needed to stick to the story?

I almost said something, almost asked Zanny about it right there on top of the Space Needle, but I didn't. I just had a feeling I shouldn't.

I had a feeling she'd act like I was being weird, I was being crazy, I was being paranoid. And maybe I was.

I ate my burger. Then I kept my mouth shut.

Until now, anyway.

Now I can tell you that, even though it's not part of the story America wants to hear, Mom was the reason I jumped that fence behind our house and landed in the rose bush. I couldn't deal with Zanny hearing about Mom and telling me how sorry she was, couldn't deal with her putting her arm around me, couldn't deal with her sympathy.

And I couldn't deal with Gene calling me Demetrius in that annoying, fake stage voice.

I got a part, apparently. Demetrius. Who the hell was Demetrius? And how the hell was I going to deal with that voice of Gene's for the next ten weeks, in math class, in the hallway, at lunch?

"Did you get problem 27, good Demetrius?"

"Hold up, honest Demetrius."

"Are you going to eat that, kind Demetrius?"

You shouldn't be able to say that kind of stuff to someone whose mother just ran away from home.

What the hell? I shook my head, amazed she could do this to us. I was walking along the abandoned-looking bike path toward the center of town, the whole trail covered with wet leaves soaking my sneakers, lonely, half-naked trees crowding in on either side. This was my mother we were talking about, running away from home. We're not that kind of family. We had Jake, smoking pot, occasionally getting beat up by someone for stealing a girlfriend, but that was about it. Dad was normal as dirt. My sister Robin was a little radical, but she still graduated from college in three and a half years. Even Mom was basically run-of-the-mill. She'd taken some art history courses; she'd complained about her job; she'd joined that hippie women's group that went around holding candlelight vigils for whales and endangered insects.

But she'd never threatened to walk out.

She'd never even thrown anything. Or locked herself in the bathroom.

She took only a part-time job when we were younger so she could meet us as we got off the bus. Sat us down and fed us milk and cookies and talked to us, really found out about our day. Took us to plays, museums, concerts. Folded Jake's shirts in half, the way he liked, and folded mine lengthwise, the way I liked.

Now, all of a sudden, she was gone?

A gust of wind came along, sending leaves flying. My teeth chattered, and I dug my hands deeper in my pockets, wishing I'd grabbed a jacket on my way out.

Where did Mom go, anyway? Did her hippie friends have a hideout someplace up on a mountain? Had Mom been planning this? Did she spend the fall carting supplies up for the winter? Firewood? She'd better have plenty of damn firewood because she hates the cold.

My teeth went into rapid-fire chatter and I tried to breathe and calm them down, wondering what the symptoms were for hypothermia. It was only another mile or so to the center of town, but what if I went into convulsions and fell off the path? With the leaves falling, they might not find me until March.

Although why that would matter once I was dead, I had no idea.

The rain was getting heavier than a drizzle again. I could see individual drops against the gray sky.

What was Mom thinking? That's what I didn't get. I knew she'd been unhappy, knew she and Dad had been fighting a lot in their quiet, don't-let-the-kids-know way. I even knew she'd been seeing a therapist.

But running away? What was the point of that?

I needed to talk to her, needed to call her. When I got to town I'd use the pay phone outside the Brew Ha Ha to call her cell. Even if she didn't answer I could leave a message.

"Mom, I don't understand. I thought you loved us."

Something cheap like that. Or I could call and be nice.

"I miss you, Mom, but I know you wouldn't leave us unless you absolutely had to."

That was just another cheap shot, though, disguised as being nice. But I needed to do something. Something to wake Mom up. I knew that was all Mom needed, was someone looking her in the face and saying hey.

"Hey," I said, out loud, practicing.

I walked on, kicking through the piles of red leaves littering the path. I would call Mom, that is what I'd do. I marched into town, heading straight for the Brew Ha Ha. Started jogging across Main

Street and stopped dead, right on the double yellow line. There was Dad. Inside the Brew Ha Ha, sitting at the window table facing out onto Main. He was looking up the street, then down, then back up, like he was watching a tennis match in slow motion.

Oh, God.

He was looking for Mom's car. He was hoping to see Mom's car, so he could bolt out to his car and go chasing off after her.

I stood there frozen in the middle of the street, like a squirrel waiting to see which way the car was going. Stupid squirrel. Dad looked straight ahead and saw me and looked ready to cry.

Shit.

I knew immediately that Dad was going to be worthless. Dad could not deal with this. We would have been much better off if he was the one who had run away because at least Mom would have some ideas about what to do about it. Mom would have called her friends, called the police, called the FBI. Mom might even have seen if the local news would be willing to run a story pleading with Dad to come back.

"For the children," she'd say, looking straight into the camera. "Not for me, John, but for the children."

Dad, though, would have no idea what to do. Which was why he was sitting in a coffee place instead of contacting the state police.

I dragged myself across to the Brew Ha Ha. It was hot and roasty-smelling inside, and my head immediately felt feverish, like I'd caught some fast-acting virus. I walked toward Dad, feeling like I was at Grandma's funeral all over again.

"Any word?" I asked.

Dad barely shook his head. He'd been doing his breathing. I could always tell when Dad had been practicing his Zen breathing because he always sat up straighter and moved more slowly.

"Did you call Stormy?" I asked. Stormy was the head guru of Mom's hippie friends. In a dream she'd met a goddess named Stormy Tidewater, and the next day she went about the process of legally changing her name.

"I left a message," Dad said, sounding worn-out, like this had been going on for years.

"They all know where Mom is," I told him.

"It doesn't matter," Dad said, quickly, shaking his head gently, as if trying to maintain the peace.

"Don't they have to tell us?"

Dad smiled. He reminded me of someone. Jake. When he's been smoking pot.

"Isn't there a law?" I asked Dad. "Something about missing persons?"

"Your mom's not missing," Dad said, his voice barely above a whisper. "She's gone. She's gone, and there's nothing we can do to change that. All we can do is change ourselves."

Worthless. Dad was completely worthless when he got into this spiritual zone crap. "You want anything?" I asked him, pointing to the completely empty table where Dad was sitting.

"No," he said.

Of course. Even if he wanted a cup of coffee, he'd convinced himself that it was better to not want the coffee. That's what he was like in Zen mode. Don't try to get something that you want, just try to stop wanting it.

Screw that. I went over and ordered a double latte.

This wasn't going to last. Dad wasn't a Buddhist monk, and Mom wasn't going to leave and never come back. People were over-reacting. Mom was going to be home by the end of the weekend.

I would've felt better, though, if Dad hadn't been quite so Zennish. Dad was basically a normal guy who got mad if the car broke down or his team lost in extra innings. It was usually only when things got really bad that Dad could kind of fall into this Zen coma. Where nothing was good and nothing was bad. Everything just was.

Jake had that attitude almost all the time, not caring, just letting whatever happened happen. Jake, with his superior, drug-induced calm that looked down on the rest of us mortal beings.

It made me wonder again why I didn't smoke pot. I paid for my latte and went over to sprinkle some cinnamon in it and stood there, trying to figure out why I'd never even tried pot. I knew it was partly that Jake had gotten there first, and that I didn't want to look like I was just copying him. And I knew it was also partly because I was going to wait until I got off to college.

But I also knew I was scared. I didn't feel like I knew exactly what held me together, but I suspected that it wasn't a whole heck of a lot, that it was a pretty precarious arrangement, and that pot might make me not worry so much about making everything work. I was afraid of letting whatever happened happen. What if things went wrong?

I stood there sprinkling in vanilla, nutmeg, something with the label torn off. Anything so I didn't have to go back and sit with the Zen master.

The thing was, I was around Jake. I knew how it worked when you let whatever happened happen. Things went wrong. Jake got suspended, he got arrested, he broke his hip, he got the crap beaten out of him by Janine Johnson's biker boyfriend. He couldn't drive, he lost his computer, and there wasn't a chance he was going to college.

I sipped my latte.

But he also never had to do homework, never had to worry about a test, and never had to listen to Ms. Jerkowski, our guidance counselor, talk about mapping your future. Teachers liked him, parents liked him, girls adored him. Zanny, for instance. Zanny was crazy about him. Zanny—

I put my latte down. "Oh, shit," I whispered. "Oh, shit."

I turned and looked at the back of Dad's head. I grabbed my latte and headed over to him. "We should head back, huh?" I said.

He turned. "You think so?" he asked, his eyes still calm and dumb-looking.

"Maybe Mom left a message," I said. "Jake might not have picked up."

Jake might not have picked up because Jake might not have been alone. Jake might have told Zanny and Gene about Mom, and, of course, Zanny would want to console him. Zanny was actually pretty good at consoling people. I'd seen her in action with girls, and if she was great at hugging them and whispering to them and letting them cry, with Jake she'd be a freaking Mother Theresa.

There'd be no stopping her with Jake. The consoling could go on for hours, both of them getting completely caught up in the horrible sadness of the moment.

She could lose her virginity. That's what I'd realized, in a flash, standing there with my latte. Zanny could right that second be losing her virginity, consoling Jake.

When we got to the car, Dad was still moving in slow motion, so I suggested I drive.

"Take it easy," Dad said, gently, when I pulled out and someone honked.

"OK, OK," I said, seeing a yellow light at Pine Street and accelerating through the intersection. Please don't be there. Please don't be there.

Zanny wore sexy underwear. She bragged about it, described it to me.

Why did she do that? Why did she have to tell me about her underwear?

My car was in Dad's spot in the garage, so he said to just park in Mom's. I kind of rammed the car in, and Dad threw his hands up in front of him and temporarily fell out of his trance.

"What the hell are you doing?"

"Sorry," I said, leaving the keys in the ignition and running into the kitchen. No music. I rushed through the kitchen to the front hall and listened at the foot of the stairs. Still nothing. My heart pounding, I quietly took the stairs three at a time and walked back to the door of Jake's room. Still nothing. The silence was getting to me, and I suddenly pounded on his door. It fell open. His room was a mess, but empty. OK, where'd they go?

Where the hell were they? And what clothes did they have on?

I heard a voice downstairs and cocked my head. Zanny. It was Zanny, down in the kitchen. I turned and bolted down the stairs and burst into the kitchen. Dad was standing there, alone, by the answering machine.

"Jake says not to save dinner, we'll pick something up," Zanny's voice said from the machine. "Oh, and could you tell Jimmy that rehearsal starts at nine o'clock tomorrow and he'd better not be late."

Dad turned to me. "Rehearsal?"

"I guess," I told him, and turned back around and ran upstairs and into my room and quietly shut the door. Friday night. It was freaking Friday night. Jake would blow off his curfew, and Zanny didn't even have one.

I leaned back against the door and shut my eyes.

I needed to tell her. I needed to say it.

I love you.

It wasn't like I thought it was a solution. I knew telling her wasn't going to stop her from doing whatever she was going to do with Jake. I knew it wasn't going to help any, I knew it could hurt, I knew I could end up humiliating myself, but I wanted it out there. I wanted her to know that, no matter what, I loved her, and I decided that very second that I was going to tell her first thing in the morning.

That was the plan, going to sleep. And it was still the plan, waking up, even if it didn't seem quite as brilliant as the night before. By the time I drove to school and walked into the auditorium, though, it wasn't so much of a plan as a dumb-ass idea. I sat in the third row and crossed my arms while my heart hammered away. I didn't have to do this. Just because I was idiotic enough the night before to tell myself I had to do this, that didn't mean I had to. I could just not listen. I didn't have to listen, I didn't have to—

Zanny plopped herself into the seat next to me. "We have a problem," she said, not even noticing the heart attack she just gave me.

"I need to tell you something," I said, fast, ready to get on with it.

"Never mind," she said, waving a hand. "This is more important."

"Zanny, I love—" I squinted at her, my heart holding on for dear life. "What do you mean, more important? What's more important?"

Zanny looked at me hard. "Jake," she said.

Four

The problem with running away is that life keeps going on anyway.

I ran away, escaped through the back door, and gave life a chance to happen, gave Zanny and Jake a chance to chat. It was a mistake, one of those incredibly dumb mistakes that seems so obvious later on.

It's amazing how the stupidest things in your life can end up changing things forever. If Mom hadn't forgotten her glasses that Friday morning, if I hadn't run away when Gene and Zanny showed up, if Zanny hadn't shut me up there in the auditorium when I was about to tell her I loved her. . . .

Then I wouldn't have done what I did that Monday night two months later.

That photographer would not have taken the amazing picture.

My face wouldn't have been plastered on the front page of three hundred newspapers.

Women wouldn't have been trying to kiss me.

They wouldn't have been sending me their underwear.

Zanny wouldn't have gotten so mad she spilled the beans.

And I wouldn't be locked up here in a hotel room trying to tell America the truth.

My grandmother thought everything always worked out for the best. She was really Irish and really Catholic and was a rock solid believer in everything working out for the best—you lost your job, your house blew up, your arm fell off, it didn't matter, it was all for the best. When I was six, I was on my bike and tried tossing a football to a friend riding along beside me and we collided and my bike was destroyed and my knee was cut open. Grandma was the only one there when I limped home but she wouldn't even give me a hug, she just handed me a roll of paper towels to clean up the cut and told me it was for all the best, that, who knows, the next day I might have killed myself on that bicycle.

Grandma thought even dying was all for the best. It took her four years to do it, but even the day before she died she was describing the advantages of being dead.

"There won't be anyone telling me to eat, eat, eat."

Personally, I don't know about things working out for the best. No matter how it turned out, it was a mistake to leave Zanny and Jake alone, and sitting there in the auditorium hearing Zanny talk about Jake proved it.

"What about Jake?" I asked, my voice scratching like a cactus.

Zanny took a deep breath, looking at me, dragging it out. "I think he has a drinking problem."

This didn't sound too bad to me, except for one little detail: "How did you find this out?"

Zanny ignored me. "How many beers did he have before I got there?"

"Did you guys go out drinking?"

"He had three beers while we sat at the kitchen table talking about your mom," Zanny said, flipping her hand over, as if this proved everything.

"What. And then you went to some bar?"

"Jimmy—" Zanny was suddenly exasperated. "Are you listening? He had four beers before I got there—"

"He didn't have any four beers."

"—and then three more?"

"And then what happened?"

Did you drive down to the lake? Did you kiss? Did you get wet in the rain? Did you take your clothes off?

"We went to the diner," Zanny said, shaking her head, confused. "You're missing the point."

I didn't think I was missing the point. They didn't have sex. That was the point as far as I was concerned.

"Jimmy, your brother has a drinking problem."

Oh, pleeease. He was a freaking drug addict. "Maybe he was just upset about Mom," I suggested.

"I bet you were upset about your mom, too," Zanny pointed out, "but you didn't lock yourself up in your room and start drinking all alone."

Why did I feel like this was a put-down?

"Jimmy, he needs help," Zanny said.

Oh, yeah. Jake needed help. And Zanny figured she was just the one to help him.

This was how it worked with Jake—girls wanted to save him. Jake's idiot girlfriend, Janine Johnson, started the same way, ready to pull Jake up by the scruff of his neck. She dumped her biker boyfriend—who later beat Jake up—she stopped wearing chains, stopped drinking, stopped doing drugs, all because she was determined to turn Jake around. Instead the two of them got arrested when the cops found them smoking dope in her van in the mall parking lot.

What was it with girls, anyway? Did they somehow see Jake as savable? Did these girls think he even wanted to be saved? From what? He had drugs and sex and music and now Dad's beer. Why would he even consider being saved?

"You have to do something," Zanny said.

"Me?"

"You're his twin brother."

"Like I could do something? You've got to be kidding. Hold on," I said, looking around. "Where's the hidden camera?" I looked over my shoulder and saw Mary, just standing there behind us, her arms pressed tight against her sides like she was waiting for a bus in a cold breeze.

"You OK?" I asked her.

The wrong thing to say, apparently. Tears sprouted from Mary's eyes, and her shoulders began to heave. Zanny pushed herself past my knees impatiently.

"Go get our scripts, would you, please?" she said, sounding angry, like it was all my fault. I stared as she got her arm around Mary. What was going on? What was Mary sobbing about?

Zanny waved me away with the back of her hand.

I turned my head and looked down toward the stage. I didn't see anyone handing out scripts. All I could see were theater people being theater people—Jerry Gilliam singing with Brett Pearson, Kelly

Unsworth watching Gary Jarvis fake punch Luke Rawlings, Fran Witherspoon giving Harry Quetzel a back massage.

And Gene. There was Gene, wearing this long fancy overcoat he must've borrowed from his dad, talking to Bertram Diller and Gina Giametti. There was Bertram giving Gene a high five. What was that about? They hardly knew each other. Did they strike up a friendship yesterday at the audition?

Beverly Tungsten, the stage manager, walked back toward me carrying a box. Beverly was a senior who'd been stage manager for every show since freshman year. She was this incredibly organized person who saw everything that was going on and knew everybody and helped teachers with computers and helped the administration solve cafeteria problems and tutored people in algebra and even ran the scoreboard for the basketball team.

"Hi, Jimmy," she said, reaching into her box and handing me a script of *A Midsummer Night's Dream*. "Congratulations. I can't remember anybody ever walking out on auditions and still ending up with a leading role."

Leading role? What the hell was she talking about, leading role? "I'm this Demeter guy?"

"Demetrius," Beverly said, softly, handing me a sheet listing the characters and who was playing whom. "Demetrius is the one Helena is madly in love with."

"Right, right," I said, biting my lip, looking at the list and finding Suzannah. Francis Flute. Zanny was playing Francis Flute.

"Only you ignore Helena," Beverly went on.

I nodded. "Because I'm in love with. . . ?" Francis Flute. Please, God, let it be Francis Flute.

"Hermia," Beverly said, smiling again. "You might want to read the play." She glanced over my shoulder and reached into her box and pulled out two more copies. "Looks like Mary and Suzannah need some privacy. Can you take their scripts?"

"Yeah, yeah, sure," I said, still looking at the list of characters, wondering if I got to meet Francis Flute, if I got a chance to at least dance with her, maybe.

"PEOPLE!"

Mr. Fricker appeared suddenly, center stage, clapping his hands.

"Sorry about your mom," Beverly said, turning and walking back toward the stage. I watched the back of her head. Mom? She knew about Mom? Who told her about Mom? And what did they say? It wasn't like Mom was dead. She'd be home by Monday. Why was everyone acting like it was a big deal?

"CONGREGATE!" Mr. Fricker shouted.

I stood there and watched people climb and hop and jump up on stage.

"Come on," Zanny said, sneaking up from behind and grabbing my arm. "We all need to sit in a big circle up on the stage."

I took my arm back. "How do you know what we're supposed to do?" I asked, walking behind her toward the stage.

But Zanny was ignoring me, whispering something to Mary, who was blowing her nose, looking pasty pale, like she'd just thrown up. Had she? Had she just thrown up?

Was she pregnant? Oh, my God. She's pregnant. That was why this normally very normal girl had suddenly decided to have a nervous breakdown. Mary was pregnant. And she didn't know what to do.

And she hadn't even told Gene. That was why he was acting like such a jerk, guffawing over at stage left at something Bertram said.

I didn't want to sit next to Mary, in case she burst into tears again, so I kept Zanny between us and sat down and started looking through my copy of the play, trying to figure out what the hell it was about. In the list of characters, the only thing it said about me and Lysander was "in love with Hermia." Gene was cast as Theseus, and Mary, I noticed, was Hippolyta, "betrothed to Theseus." Weird. That was just the kind of coincidence Grandma loved. God works in mysterious ways. She loved saying that. Although I didn't know what she would have said about Mary being pregnant.

"What fools these mortals be," Mr. Fricker quoted, standing in the exact center of the circle and slowly looking around at each of us.

I had to stop my eyes from rolling.

"What fools these mortals be," Mr. Fricker repeated. Shakespeare didn't repeat the line, but Fricker stood there in front of thirty-five people and said it a third time.

"What fools these mortals be."

I glanced at my watch.

"Shakespeare knows something that we forget over and over," Mr. Fricker said. Out of the corner of my eye I noticed people were really listening to him. "Love doesn't make sense. We don't love the right people, and we act like complete idiots when we do love someone."

My knee was touching Zanny's knee. I didn't know how it happened, if I moved, or she moved, but there they were, our knees, leaning against each other. I stared at Zanny's knee, her torn jeans, her pale skin peeking through.

"In the play, of course, the fairies sort everything out," Mr. Fricker said, puckering up his mouth like he'd swallowed a lemon. "Whereas the only fairies I know complicate things beyond compare."

People laughed. Louder than they needed to. If it was some other teacher, people would have accused him of being homophobic, but no one was about to accuse Mr. Fricker of being homophobic.

"We mortals don't have little fairies to look over us at night and drop love potions into our eyes while we sleep." Mr. Fricker looked around and tossed his hands. "And you know what? It sucks."

People laughed again. Ooo, how cool is that, a teacher saying sucks.

"But since we know how stupid love can be, we laugh as Helena runs through the forest chasing Demetrius, who happens to be running through the forest chasing Hermia."

The bare part of Zanny's knee was pressed against my jeans. Even through the material of my jeans I could feel the heat of her knee. I could feel heat, and I could feel. . . I didn't know how to describe it, didn't know if I was making it up, but I felt an energy flowing between our two knees. A humming, surging energy, an electric current that vibrated through my knee and into my body, and I couldn't take my eyes off our two knees, pressed against each other, couldn't pull my eyes away.

"James?"

I leapt away from Zanny's knees, as if someone had caught me doing something you should only do behind a locked door. It took a second to realize that the voice had come from behind me, that everyone had turned toward the foot of the stage, where Ms. Jerkowski, my guidance counselor, gave a smiling little wave.

"Sorry to interrupt, Mr. Fricker, but could I speak to James O'Reilly for a moment?"

I looked at her, looked at Mr. Fricker, who stood open-mouthed, like Ms. Jerkowski had just finished punching him in the face. Then he flicked his hand, dismissing me without a word. I got up, embarrassed but glad to get away from Zanny and that knee. God, what was that about?

I hopped off the stage. Ms. Jerkowski nodded with a tight smile.

"You guys work on Saturdays?" I asked her, making conversation. I always thought guidance counselors were supposed to make you feel comfortable, but with Ms. Jerkowski there were always these awkward silences, like what happens with sober adults at parties. "I didn't know you guys worked on Saturdays."

"Sometimes," Ms. Jerkowski said. "Shall we walk?"

"Uhh—" I looked up at the stage at Mr. Fricker, like I couldn't stand the thought of missing what he said.

"It'll just take a second," Ms. Jerkowski reassured me, turning toward the back of the auditorium and looking down to check on her breasts. Ms. Jerkowski always wore tight blouses that showed off her breasts, but she was constantly checking to make sure nothing was accidentally exposed.

Walking toward the back of the auditorium, I knew what this was about. I knew Ms. Jerkowski had somehow heard about Mom, and I knew she was going to ask all sorts of miserable questions in order to determine just how traumatized I was. And I knew I needed to act friendly about the idiotic questions because if I told her to get lost, she would assume I was not adjusting well, that I might be emotionally disturbed. I knew you need to play along with counselors until you can get rid of them.

And that's what I did. Even though I knew this was ridiculous, even though I knew Mom was going to be back in a day or two, when we got out in the hallway and Ms. Jerkowski started in about how sorry she was, I nodded my head and agreed it was hard and agreed I needed to talk to someone and agreed to stop by her office anytime I wanted.

"Now how about your classes?" Ms. Jerkowski asked, scribbling something on her clipboard.

"What do you mean?" I was trying to figure out the right answer here.

Ms. Jerkowski flipped a page over on her clipboard, suddenly very busy. "Are you interested in transferring out of any classes?"

"Well, uh—" Was this my chance to get out of Mr. Grout's pre-calculus class?

Ms. Jerkowski buried her face in her clipboard. "Ms. Farling's, for instance?"

"Ms. Farling?" What was she talking about? I didn't get it. "She's a really good teacher."

"Of course she is," Ms. Jerkowski admitted. "I just thought. . . you might want to get out of her class."

I didn't know the right answer here. "Why?"

"Uh—well, uh—I guess—I guess—The workload, maybe. I don't know."

What the hell was going on? What the hell was she hiding? My mind jumped back to the parking lot, to Ms. Farling crying. What was going on with Ms. Farling? That involved me?

"Well, all righty, then," Ms. Jerkowski said, quickly.

"It might help if I could get out of Mr. Grout's class," I suggested to her.

"Oh, I don't think so," she said, checking off one final thing on the clipboard, suddenly in a hurry. "Mr. Grout will do just fine. And I'd better get you back to rehearsal before Mr. Fricker kicks my butt."

Ms. Jerkowski practically shoved me back into the auditorium, where Mr. Fricker was still up there on stage, talking to his circle of actors. I climbed up there and rejoined the circle, avoiding Zanny's eyes.

"Why would he write this play?" Mr. Fricker was asking. "Why would William Shakespeare let fairies trivialize the passions of these people? Why—"

Zanny elbowed me and pointed to something she'd scribbled on the back of her script. I didn't want to look, didn't want to read it. She was going to ask about the knees. She saw me going into that trance about our knees and she wanted to know what was wrong with me. She wanted to know what was going on, she wanted to know why I was getting weird about a couple of knees.

I rubbed my forehead like I didn't notice anything, but Zanny just elbowed me harder. I had no choice. I looked.

We need to talk.

I blinked. This was bad. I couldn't get away, couldn't just sneak out the back door. I looked back at Fricker. Maybe if I just ignore her. I can ignore her. I'll just ignore her.

She elbowed me again. I looked down and saw her underline *talk*.

I swallowed. Took her pen and wrote on the back of my script:
About what?

She gave me a look. She knew. Oh, God, she knew. Zanny took her pen back and I closed my eyes, panic and joy filling me from the inside out. She knew. Thank God. It was over. She knew, she knew. I held my breath as I opened my eyes and read.

We need to find your mom.

Five

Why did I want her to know? Why was I so happy when I thought she'd figured it out? Was I sick? She liked Jake. She would've laughed in my face. Our friendship would've been over.

In Kansas on our promotional tour we met an old man with a limp who said when he was in the army a woman pointed a gun at him and warned him not to say he loved her or she'd shoot. The bullet plowed into an artery in his leg and he almost bled to death before she could get him to the hospital.

In Kentucky we met a woman who owned a diner. The cook left town because she told him she loved him.

In Arizona a thirty-year-old guy told us about getting beaten up every day of his senior year of high school because he told another guy on the football team that he loved him.

What is it about love that makes it so stupid? That makes you want to blab? That makes it like a truth serum, so you want to tell the world everything?

Which is not exactly what Zanny does in *Love Doesn't Grow on Trees.* Zanny's more interested in the story than in truth serums, than in telling the world everything. She says on page 22 that she had a sense on the first day of rehearsal that I was more traumatized by my mom leaving than I was letting on. She says she knew, for my sake, that we needed to find her.

What is she talking about? Me? She thought I was the traumatized one? Then why was Jake the only one she was talking about? Why was she having a nervous breakdown about Jake's drinking problem?

I wasn't traumatized. I was positive everyone was overreacting, that Mom would be back by Sunday night, that in two days everything would be back to normal. Everything was going to be fine, I knew it.

So I just thought it was annoying when I got home from rehearsal and my sister Robin was there in the kitchen, emptying the dishwasher.

"What are you doing here?"

Robin stopped for a second, then kept grabbing glasses and plonking them into the cupboard overhead. "You know, Dad warned me you'd be a pain in the ass. I told him, 'Dad, come on, he's not a moron, he'll appreciate the extra help.'"

"What. You're going to do my homework?" I grabbed a glass from the cupboard and headed for the fridge.

"For your information, little brother. . . ."

That was enough, that was all I needed. I was willing to put up with "for your information" because I knew Robin loved giving everyone information, loved informing people, but the "little brother" put it over the top. I was almost seventeen years old and a foot taller than she was. Enough with the little brother business.

She claimed Dad asked her to come, and, deciding that her family needed her (like we needed holes in our heads), she caught the next flight east. (The last time Dad had talked to her, she'd been saving trees somewhere by delivering supplies to people who actually lived in trees so logging companies couldn't cut the trees down.)

I couldn't believe Dad was overreacting like this. Sending for Robin, as if we couldn't deal without Mom for a couple of days.

I poured some milk and went into the family room and logged on to check my e-mail. Nothing from Zanny, but some lady called nakedxxx78921 wanted me to peruse 35,000 absolutely free naked pictures. I didn't want my older sister walking in on me looking at thousands of naked women, and I knew if I was going to look at naked women I'd better get my math homework done first, so I got out my math book and sat back down at the computer table in the family room and opened it up.

There it was. The letter from Mom. With "Jimmy" scribbled across it. I swallowed and just looked at it for a long while before reaching for it.

Then the phone rang.

I jumped. Mom? Was it Mom? I picked up before the second ring. "Hello?"

"Can you tell me why Mary just hung up on me?"

It was Gene, who apparently didn't know his girlfriend was pregnant.

"She has been acting so bizarre lately," he went on, not waiting for an answer. "Two weeks ago was incredible, was amazing, was the most fantastic experience of my life—"

Please don't tell me you had sex. I realize you had sex, but please don't say it.

"—and now she's hanging up on me."

"What did you say to her?"

"I didn't say anything," Gene claimed.

"Nothing?"

"We were talking about the movie."

The four us were supposed to go see *Oh, Him* at the mall that night.

"Mary was saying the woman falls in love with the neighbor all because of these notes he slips under her door, and I said that sounded dumb."

"And she hung up on you?" I didn't get why saying a movie is dumb would annoy a pregnant woman, but Dad claimed that when Mom was pregnant, breathing could annoy her.

"I'm telling you, two weeks ago was unbelievable," Gene repeated.

"Yeah, yeah," I said. "We'll meet you guys at six."

I got off the phone in a hurry, and then realized I was actually holding in my hand the letter from Mom. The Jimmy letter. I took a deep breath and opened the envelope.

It was bad. I only read it once, and skimming over some of the words, then put it back in the envelope, and just sat there.

Mom wasn't coming back. Something had happened the day before, and she didn't want to talk about it, but we needed to understand that she and Dad were splitting up. She couldn't see us for a couple of days, please don't e-mail her, please don't try to find her, just know that she was fine and loved us more than blah, blah, blah.

I stood up, walked around, sat back down. What the hell? I went up to my room and put on my boom box and turned it up loud. Grabbed a yellow tennis ball and walked around in a circle, bouncing the ball off the wall over my desk. What the hell happened? That she would just leave us?

I went back downstairs, did my math homework, finished *Heart of Darkness* for English, thought about Mom, thought about Mom and Dad, set the table for dinner and ate it, tofu and all, and had my plate scraped off in and in the dishwasher before Zanny showed up for the movie.

"Robin!"

"Zanny!"

They gave each other a big hug and talked about saving trees. I kept looking at the clock on the microwave.

"What is Robin doing here?" Zanny asked me, before I could even get the front door closed.

"What? Nothing."

"She flies three thousand miles for nothing?"

"I guess."

Zanny didn't bring it up again until the lights went down in the movie theater.

"What's the deal with your mom?"

I pointed to the preview. "Can we watch here?"

Gene was right about the movie. It was idiotic, the woman neighbor not realizing she loved the guy neighbor until she was at his wedding, where he was marrying another woman because she had the same hair as his neighbor.

I loved it. I actually had to fight back tears when the neighbors got together at the end, but when we went to Starbucks afterward and Mary and Zanny started talking about it, I just shrugged and looked over at the people walking in and out of Macy's.

Zanny told Mary and Gene about my sister Robin, how she was going to be home for a while. They both thought it was great.

"Robin loves this sort of thing," I said. "Saving the trees. Saving the Gila monster. Saving the family. She lives for this kind of thing, for being able to come to the rescue."

"So what's wrong with that?" Zanny asked. "So Robin likes helping people. Is that a bad thing?"

"It's not bad. It's just—" I looked back at Gene. "Do you remember how she used to try to talk us out of Shoot Em Up?" I looked at Mary. "Gene and I invented a game called Shoot Em Up where we came up with cool ways of dying when we were shot. Robin used to freak out because we were pretending to shoot each other. Even though we wanted to get shot. That was the point of the game. To get shot."

"And you're trying to tell us Robin's the weird one?" Zanny asked.

Mary laughed. Too loud. Gene and I looked at her. Mary was moving her hands like they were brand new and she didn't know how to work them.

When were they going to tell Gene? If Mary was pregnant, shouldn't Gene know about it? I looked over at him. God, he was going to flip. What about school? What about Tufts? What about his entire freaking life?

"Robin's a good person," Zanny said. "That ought to count for something."

"She threw out Dad's beer," I told them. "She found a couple of empty cans up in Jake's room and told Dad he couldn't have beer in the house anymore. Then she went through every cupboard and found an old bottle of Bacardi that no one even knew was there, and she poured it down the sink. A full bottle. Unopened."

Zanny cleared her throat. "I think it's great someone's trying to help Jake."

Oh, God. "She's out-momming Mom," I said.

"Then don't you think it would be good if we go find your real mom?" Zanny asked.

She wouldn't let it go, this idea of tracking down Mom. She thought it was critical to Jake, that he was at a crossroads and needed Mom to be there. To help him feel loved. Without Mom around, she thought Jake could end up doing something really stupid. I wanted to point out to her that Jake was always doing something really stupid, but Zanny was still acting like it was the end of the world.

"If we found your mom we could at least tell her about Jake and let her decide what to do."

"Tell her what?" I asked. "That Jake drank some beer? You don't think my mom knows that Jake drinks beer?"

"So she'll decide she doesn't need to come home," Zanny said. "Is there anything wrong with that?"

"Zanny?"

I looked away. Had to look away. Her hair was falling over her right eye, and I was full of the movie we'd just seen, so full of what could happen, what should happen, so aware of Zanny's dark eyes that my heart lurched, like a train pulling out of the station.

"You guys want to head down to the food court?" Gene asked.

I saw Mary and Zanny look at each other.

"Actually," Zanny announced, "Mary and I have to do some shopping."

I knew it! Mary was pregnant. Mary was pregnant, and she and Zanny were keeping it from Gene, and now they were going to go buy. . . What the hell would they be buying? I glanced discreetly at Mary's belly. Maternity clothes? Already?

Zanny tapped my arm. "Do you think you could give Gene a ride home, Jim?"

"Why?" I asked. "We could just hang out at the food court and wait for you."

Under the table, Zanny stepped on my foot. "It's going to take us a while."

Why? What were they buying?

Were there things pregnant women needed that were so gross no one ever talked about them? God, I didn't even want to think about it.

"We can go hang out down at the arcade," Gene suggested.

Again, Mary and Zanny looked at each other. Why didn't they just say it? Why didn't they just tell Gene that Mary was pregnant and get it over with? Unless. . . maybe they didn't know, not for sure. Maybe they were buying a pregnancy test, and they planned on taking it back to Mary's house and finding out right away, one way or the other.

I winced, trying to shake this image in my mind of Mary peeing onto a stick. Back in middle school Freddy Watman saw his sister burying something deep in one of their trash cans, so of course he went looking for it and found the box for a pregnancy test. He brought the instructions in to show everyone—instructions that had a little drawing of just how to position yourself over the stick. It was more than I would ever want to know.

"We have no idea how long it's going to take," Zanny said, looking at me.

"I don't care," Gene said, shrugging, flipping his thumb at me. "Do you mind waiting?"

Zanny pressed the edge of her heel into my foot.

"Ow."

Gene looked at me. "What's wrong with you?"

I shifted my feet under my chair. "I've got a pain in my ass."

He laughed. "What?"

"Anyone want some gum?" Zanny asked. "Jim, you want to walk over with me?"

Oh, yeah, real smooth. I almost said something, but I wanted to know what the hell was going on, so I kept my mouth closed and stood up.

Mary looked at her watch. "Are you watching the time?" she asked Zanny.

"I'm watching the time," Zanny told her, nodding. "The time is just fine. We'll be back in three minutes. Let's go," she said, grabbing the sleeve of my jean jacket and pulling me along.

It felt like it had been so long, years maybe, since I had actually been alone with Zanny, and just walking out of Starbucks with her, just getting a teasing scent of her herbal shampoo made me go quiet. Looking at her, she was so. . . bright. Just this moment, the two of us walking out into the mall, looking at each other, her eyes dark and piercing, the two of us connecting with a look—the moment seemed like something that I would remember the rest of my life.

"You're such an asshole," she said.

"What?"

"Can't you take a hint?"

"Not when I have no idea what the hell is going on."

"You need to get Gene out of here."

"You've got to be kidding me," I said. "You're not going to tell me why?"

Zanny shook her head. "Just leave it alone. OK?"

"What are you shopping for?"

Now she laughed. What the hell was so funny? "Things," she said.

"Like—?"

"Girl things, Jim."

I could tell by the way she said it that she thought that would scare me away. Tampons, yeast infections, or maybe something I'd never even heard of. "Yeah? Like what?" I asked, calling her bluff.

Zanny turned and squinted at me, surprised. Impressed.

God, it felt good. Like she'd leaned over and kissed me on the cheek. "I know what's going on," I told her.

Zanny laughed. "Oh, I don't think so."

My confidence was not shaken. "Oh, I think so."

Zanny kept laughing. "What do you want to bet?"

"A kiss," I said.

That stopped her cold. "What?" Zanny asked, standing there, looking at me.

What the hell was I thinking? "Not—" Oh, shit. Think, think. "One of those, you know—A jumbo chocolate kiss."

Zanny stared at me a long time, suspicious. "Fine," she said.

"Fine," I said, back.

Zanny started walking again but sighed like she was taking pity on me. "Look, Jimmy. You really don't know what's going on. Mary and I have something to do. Just forget about it and take Gene home, would you, please?"

"What do you have to do?" I asked, bursting with confidence. I had it. I had this bet won.

"I can't tell you," Zanny said.

"She's pregnant," I said, positive, beyond-a-doubt sure.

Zanny stopped walking again and stared at me, her eyes big. How did I know?

Yes! I got it!

Zanny shook her head. "Are you INSANE?"

Six

Zanny loves that story, loves talking about that night at the mall, when I was so absolutely positive Mary was pregnant and I was so absolutely positively wrong. On the talk-shows it always gets a laugh. Stupid Jim. What a moron. What an idiot.

I hate thinking about that night at the mall, but not because I was an idiot. Being an idiot's OK. It's being a jerk that bothers me. And I was an incredible jerk that night.

I tried to explain that on a radio show in Des Moines, and Zanny sat there waving her hands, shaking her head, trying to get me to shut up. It wasn't part of the story, it wasn't what people wanted to hear, that I was a jerk. She even had Mr. Nelson call me that night at the hotel.

"Look, kid," he said, "save the confessions for your priest."

"I don't go to church."

"No?" Mr. Nelson seemed to consider this. "What about Doug?"

"Doug?"

"Dr. Hackinfire."

Dr. Hackinfire. My psychologist. In order to get out of jail after the tree mess, I had to agree to have twenty sessions with a therapist. As soon as Mr. Nelson heard about it, he hooked me up with this big shot psychologist guy out in Hollywood, Dr. Hackinfire.

"What do you think we're paying him for, kid? Confess to Doug in private, and out in the real world, stay on message."

That was Mr. Nelson's favorite expression. On message. It was what politicians were always supposed to do—talk only about the stuff they wanted to talk about so they could get their message across. For me, on message meant I could say anything I wanted, just as long as I sounded like a nice kid. That was the point, that was the message: nice kid. It was OK for America to think I was dumb, just as long as they believed in their heart that I was this really nice kid.

That I was a jerk, that I betrayed my friend that night, didn't enter into the picture. It was the type of thing Zanny and I were never supposed to talk about. As a matter of fact, in *Love Doesn't Grow on Trees,* Zanny doesn't mention that I came back to the mall that night. As far as her book is concerned, she asks me if I'm insane, and I go take Gene home. Not a word about me driving like a maniac, taking Gene home, so I could get back to the mall.

But that's what happened. Fifteen minutes after Zanny asked me if I was insane, I was accelerating up Main Street, trying to get Gene home as fast as possible.

"You hungry at all?" he asked, looking over at the McDonald's on Meriden.

"Not really," I told him, beeping at the pickup truck in front of us because the old man inside didn't seem to notice that the light had turned green.

"Want to stop at the Brew Ha Ha for a latte?"

"I'm pretty tired," I said, punching the steering wheel because we'd just missed the light at Stonehouse. Now that I knew what was going on, I couldn't wait to get back to the mall. Zanny knew that was going to happen. She knew that as soon as I found out what was going on, there was no way I was going to want to leave, so before she told me, she made me swear on my grandmother's grave that I'd take Gene home immediately.

"I'll treat," Gene said. "A latte and a Krispy Kreme."

Gene knew Krispy Kremes were like a drug to me. Only not tonight, I wasn't interested.

"No, thanks," I said, biting my lip, sitting forward, glancing at the clock on the dashboard.

Gene chuckled, then guffawed. "I think Mary might be embarrassed," he said. And when I didn't say anything, he went on. "By something she did two weeks ago."

Yeah, yeah, yeah, I already knew all about what Mary had done two weeks ago, and, frankly, I thought it sucked that Gene was willing to talk about oral sex just so I'd hang out with him. If your girlfriend does something like that, you don't go around bragging about it. You go around shaking your head, amazed at your luck, but you keep your mouth shut about it.

Especially when she's not doing it because she likes you but because she feels guilty.

Zanny explained to me what happened when we were back at the mall.

"What?" I said, loud enough for some women walking into Talbot's to look over their shoulders.

Mary was Catholic. Her father forced her to go to church, her mother said the rosary during Lent. I would've bet they thought that even a married woman shouldn't be doing what Mary did.

"She only did it because she felt guilty," Zanny said.

I shook my head, confused. "You're telling me she felt guilty, so she gave Gene—"

"She's meeting someone here tonight," Zanny said, cutting me off. "A guy."

"What? What guy?"

"Someone she met on the Internet."

"What are you talking about?" I asked, stopping dead right there outside the bookstore. "You're telling me Mary met someone on the Internet, and now she's agreed to actually see him?"

"Shhh," Zanny said. "At first I thought she was kidding."

"The Internet? What, does she want to die?"

"Jimmy, calm down."

"This is crazy! The Internet?"

Zanny nodded. "I know, I know. I said the same thing."

"But what? Now you think it's OK? Oh, sure. Go ahead, meet this total freak, what do I care?"

"He's not a total freak," Zanny said. "They've been e-mailing every day for over a year."

"And that doesn't make him some bald, middle-aged pervert?"

"Will you calm down?"

"What are you talking about? This is like something they show in health! Girl Who Met Guy on Internet Found in Three Wastepaper Baskets."

"Jimmy. She hired a private detective."

I looked at Zanny. I didn't even know you could do that, that a sixteen-year-old could, all on her own, hire a private detective. Zanny wouldn't tell me how much Mary paid, but the guy went all the way up to Connecticut and talked to the kid and even a couple of his teachers.

"So she hires a private detective to check this guy out, and then she decides to give Gene a—?" Of course. The only reason a Catholic girl would do something like that. Never because she wanted to. Only out of guilt.

Now I was stuck inside a car with Gene, who wouldn't stop hinting around about it. "I don't know what got into her," he said, laughing again.

I slammed on the brakes and pointed at the car in front of us. "Do you believe this guy? Stopping on a yellow? Who stops on a yellow?"

"I gave up even mentioning it," Gene said. "I figured I'd have to wait until we got to college before, you know—"

My cell phone started playing *Jingle Bells*.

Oh, thank God. Robin had gone out that very afternoon and gotten us all cell phones because she thought we should all be able to contact each other at all times. As if Mom running away from home was some kind of terrorist crisis. I thought Robin was crazy, but now I was glad to have my dumb little cell phone. Anything to shut Gene up.

"Hello?"

"Jingle Bells" kept playing.

"You want to hit the top button," Gene said.

"I know."

"The green one."

"I know," I said, hitting the green button. "Hello?"

"James?" It was Robin.

"What's up?"

"Have you seen Jake?" she asked, her voice choppy, staticky. How much did we pay for these cell phones, anyway?

"You lost Jake?" I asked.

"What?" Robin sounded completely stressed out. "I can't even hear you."

"Because we're using these cheap cell phones."

"What? What are you saying? James, are you on the road? Are you driving?"

"I'm allowed to drive, Robin."

"Not when you're on a cell phone, you idiot. Now pull over."

"What are you talking about?"

"Jimmy, it is against the law in this state to drive while using a cell phone."

"Since when?" I didn't know for sure, but I had my doubts.

"You need to pull over," Robin said. "Now."

"Robin. I'm in a hurry."

"Why are you in a hurry?" Gene asked.

I ignored him. "What did you say?" I asked, into the phone, just for cover.

"James?" It was Robin again. "James, Dad is standing right here, and he says it is not safe to drive and talk on the cell phone at the same time."

"Fine," I said, looking up and seeing the light turn green. I hit the little red button on the phone, hanging up on Robin, and took off through the green light. Hey, she was the one who said it was dangerous to speak on a cell phone and drive at the same time.

"Why are you in a hurry?" Gene asked again.

I stared through the windshield. "What," I said. "I feel like I'm going to fall asleep any second." It was a bad lie, but I kept my eyes on the car in front of us, hoping the silence meant Gene was buying it.

"What's going on?" he asked, finally.

"What?" I asked. I wished Robin would call back on the cell phone.

"Something's going on," Gene said, almost whining, "and Zanny told you what it is and you're not telling me."

"What are you talking about?" I asked, trying to think, trying to figure out what the hell I could say. Besides the truth, that his girl-friend was back at the mall, about to meet the love of her life.

Gene didn't say anything for a long while, and I thought maybe I could get away with just keeping my mouth shut, but it didn't last. "I thought you were my friend," he said, softly.

Oh, God. Did Gene hear that in some schlocky movie? I pulled up to the next light and sagged in my seat. I had to say something, I knew I had to say something, and instead of just telling him the truth, I somehow decided to be a complete jerk.

"It's a Christmas present," I said.

"It's what?" Gene asked, his hopes rising.

I couldn't believe I was doing this. "A Christmas present. They're getting a Christmas present."

What a jerk. What an asshole. I felt sick as soon as I said it, but not sick enough to tell him the truth.

"A present for me?" Gene asked. He sounded like a little kid. Sounded like a puppy. Sounded like a little kid getting a puppy.

"Gene—"

"What is it? What's she getting me?"

"Gene—"

"Just tell me what it is."

It's some guy Mary met on the Internet, I should have told him. Some guy who lives in freaking Connecticut she's been instant messaging for over a year. Some guy she and Zanny are meeting at the mall. . . three minutes ago.

"Gene, just shut up, would you, please?" I drove even faster now, just wanting to get rid of this idiot friend I had just completely betrayed. This idiot friend who, when we got to his house, patted me on the shoulder and thanked me before getting out of the car.

Oh, God.

I sped back to the mall, waiting to be punished, waiting for some old lady to run out in front of the car and send me to jail for vehicular homicide. Something had to happen. You don't totally betray a friend and not pay for it. I would not have been surprised if a truck had appeared out of nowhere and rolled over on top of me and sent me straight to hell, where I belonged, but instead I made it to the mall parking lot and started looking for a space.

It's not a good thing to be in a hurry to find a parking space at the mall on a Saturday night before Christmas. I nearly ran over a cop directing traffic, then nearly slammed into the side of an SUV.

Neil Gannon.

That was name of this guy, this guy Mary was meeting. Neil Gannon. Zanny told me his name, told me he came from Fairview, Connecticut.

"Connecticut?" I said. Like it was a foreign country, a rich, snobby country, full of kids with blond hair who wore sweaters.

This Neil guy was driving all the way from Connecticut, and he had never even seen a picture of Mary.

"They thought it'd be more romantic," Zanny explained.

"Romantic? You mean stupid."

"You're just jealous," Zanny said.

"What if the guy turns out to weigh three hundred pounds?"

"You're jealous," Zanny said.

I stared at her. Imagined living in Connecticut and sending her e-mails for a year. And getting e-mails back, asking me if I'd like to get together, asking me if I'd be willing to drive down to New Jersey so we could meet.

Zanny was right. I was foaming at the mouth jealous.

And I was dying to see this guy. Dying to see what happened, what he and Mary thought, what they said, seeing each other for the first time.

I finally found a space and ran into the mall, which was amazingly bright and loud with *"Deck the Halls"* echoing off the glass ceiling and the four-foot snowflakes hanging all over the place. A Santa was ringing a bell, people were leaving with four or five shopping bags—it was actually kind of Christmassy, in a shallow, commercialized sort of way.

The Starbucks was hidden, coming from this side of the mall. I went around and came toward it from the other direction so I could watch before I got close. If Mary saw me, I was dead—Zanny had already told me she'd put a knife in my chest. I laughed when she said it, but luckily she didn't get the joke.

"Can I help you?"

I was cutting through one of those corner jewelry stores, and the chicken-necked old lady behind the counter must have thought I looked pretty damn guilty, moving in slow motion like that.

"No, thanks," I said, trying to be polite but not taking my eyes off the front of Starbucks. I didn't see them, so I walked slowly, casually, out of the jewelry store, and cut straight across to the stores on the Starbucks side of the walkway. I looked in store windows as I crept, step by step, closer to Starbucks. Sneakers, leather jackets, women's clothes, one of those trendy places where the mannequins had breasts with nipples. Zanny and her two lover friends weren't sitting at any of the outside tables, so I crossed back over to the other side of the walkway and headed right into a luggage store and stood inside looking out over at Starbucks. No Zanny, no Mary, no sweaters.

"Can I help you?"

I looked over my shoulder and saw a salesperson who couldn't have been more than twenty-five. I couldn't believe she was already doing the harass-the-teenager bit. Traitor. I just gave her a look of disgust and walked out. It didn't matter, anyway, Zanny was gone, Mary was gone.

"Shhhhhit," I whispered to myself, walking straight across over to Starbucks. Where the hell would they go? If I were meeting Zanny for the very first time in our lives, where would I take her? Where do you go in a mall? When you're madly in love with someone? The freaking Disney Store?

I got a tall latte, fully caffeinated, forget about sleep, I needed a lift, a life, something. I'd just betrayed one of my best friends to get back to the mall to see Mary with this guy from Connecticut, and they weren't even there.

I sat down at one of the tables outside, looking left, looking right, hoping maybe they'd just walk by. Did Mary like to window-shop?

I crossed my arms and looked over at the Polar train ride they set up in the courtyard every Christmas. Most of the little kids were riding alone, but there were a couple of parents on the ride, too, their legs stuffed in front of them, their knees in the air like they were basketball players. The kid in the front car was yanking hard on the rope that blew the whistle.

Wooooooooooo. Wooooooooooo.

It was an incredibly annoying sound, but the problem was, his family was over on the other side, clapping and encouraging him to keep pulling on the rope.

Woooooooooooooo. Woooooooooooooooooooooooooo.

It was getting on my nerves. Then it got worse when I realized it wasn't his family, across the way, encouraging him.

It was Zanny. And Mary. And Neil.

There he was. Neil Gannon. A normal-looking guy. Tall, like Gene, but perfectly normal-looking. No sweater, even.

The three of them were hollering to the kid and pulling down on imaginary ropes, trying to get him to imitate them. They looked like they were having a blast, and I felt something pull at me inside. I watched Zanny talking to Mary and laughing and holding onto the white picket fence, and I felt this push on my chest, this pressure that wasn't painful, particularly, but that made me want to take pictures. Or draw. I would have drawn Zanny standing there, dropping her head on Mary's shoulder, laughing, if I'd known how to draw.

Woooooooooooooooooooo. Woooooooooooooooooooooooooooooooo.

Or poetry. I could really have written a poem about Neil and Mary looking at each other, and maybe a whole other poem about Zanny's happiness, I could have written a long poem about watching from a distance the happiness of the girl you love. I was glad I didn't have a pen. I had a feeling I could really do some damage with a pen, could write one of those angst poems that would, as Ms. Farling always said, give poetry a bad name.

Everything slowed down, watching them, watching her. It made me breathe differently. And just look at Zanny Manning in a way I hadn't before. She wasn't that pretty, she really wasn't. But there was stuff going on inside her that I'd never seen in anybody else I'd ever met. We'd talked, we'd said words, we traded looks that made me see how she thought, how her mind just worked differently from anyone else I had ever known.

And I appreciated it. I sat there with my latte and looked across and realized I appreciated Suzannnah Manning in a way nobody else did.

And I felt an ache, a real ache down through the center of my body. I wanted to tell her. I wanted her to know. Just to know there was someone who really did get her, who appreciated her in the way she deserved to be appreciated. I wanted her to know that. I sat back, looking at her, wanting her to know there was someone—it happened to be me, but that didn't matter—I wanted her to know that there was someone who loved her the way she was supposed to be loved.

I sat back, watching, watching and breathing.

And suddenly I realized.

Looking at Neil Gannon, looking at Neil and Mary, my heart leapt up, because—of course! Of course there was a way it could happen.

Of course there was a way I could tell Zanny.

Seven

OK, so here I am in San Diego, and apparently I'm crazy.

I just finished typing up the last chapter and decided to take a break and turned on the headline news. They had a little blurb about me locking myself up here, threatening to blow my brains out if anyone tried to come in. According to them, I'm completely loony. Paranoid, suicidal, possible drug abuser, the whole bit. Possible drug abuser? Apparently Mr. Nelson is going all out. I switched over to CNN and left it on while I made a box of macaroni and cheese in the microwave, and, as I was waiting, stuffing my face with chips, I saw Zanny on the TV and turned up the sound. I couldn't believe it. She was near tears, talking about me. It was incredible. I got goose bumps watching her, listening to her talk about how she knew I was struggling, knew I'd been having a hard time ever since I lost my computer in Minneapolis, the computer containing the only copy of the book I was supposed to be writing.

I squinted at the television screen. "Zanny—what are you talking about?"

I didn't lose the computer. It was stolen. Right out of my room. As I was sleeping.

Zanny knew that. She knew the computer was stolen. She knew—

I sat back very slowly, realizing what was going on.

She's thinks I'm crazy.

Zanny thinks I'm crazy. She thinks the security guys in Minneapolis were right, that it was impossible for someone to sneak into my room, that I had somehow misplaced the computer, that I was confused.

That's not what happened, though.

What happened was, we were in Minneapolis, at that nice hotel with the flat-screen TVs. And I was so fed up with Mr. Nelson hounding me about finishing the book that I actually talked about it in my therapy session over the phone with Dr. Hackinfire.

"Mmm," was all he said. And then, very casually, "Well, and how's the writing going? What have you written about so far?"

That's what he asked me, like he was just curious. And I made the mistake, the gigantic mistake of telling him. Of telling him I was writing about Mom. About Robin. About Jake.

"Jake? Really? You've been writing about your brother?"

"Well, him and Zanny, yeah," I said. Idiot! Complete idiot.

"Hmmmm. I see. That's interesting." Dr. Hackinfire seemed to be fascinated, all of a sudden. "And have you shown your work to Mr. Nelson?"

"Uh—Well, no."

"Hmmm," Dr. Hackinfire said, his voice calm, soft. "Why not?"

Was he crazy? Did he think I was going to show that stuff to Mr. Nelson? When I knew it would make Mr. Nelson freak? The day Zanny sent Mr. Nelson the first draft of *Love Doesn't Grow on Trees*, Mr. Nelson had a conference call with the two of us and told us talking about Jake was strictly forbidden. Just don't bring him up, period. Jake clouded things up, he said. We were supposed to talk about Zanny, and we were supposed to talk about me. If anyone asked about Jake, we were supposed to change the subject.

So I knew writing about Zanny being madly in love with Jake was not exactly what Mr. Nelson was looking for. Just to be safe, I kept my laptop with me at all times, wouldn't let anybody else carry it, wouldn't let even Zanny see what I was writing. Hackinfire had to be kidding if he thought I'd even consider showing it to Mr. Nelson.

Turns out I didn't have a choice.

I woke up the next day after my phone call with Dr. Hackinfire, and my laptop was gone. Stolen. Someone had snuck right into my hotel room, while I was sleeping. The hotel security guys were horrified, said it couldn't happen, said it was physically impossible, based on the locks. Was I sure I had my laptop? Was I sure I hadn't left it somewhere? Did I ever sleep walk? Did I suffer from blackouts?

Mr. Nelson called, sounding like my grandmother, telling me maybe it was all for the best, saying maybe I needed a break—from the writing, from the tour. Maybe I'd like to take a couple of days off and go to Saint Uwell's. A resort, he called it.

At breakfast Zanny said the same thing, maybe I needed a few days off at Saint Uwell's. I watched her eat her poached egg. She had no idea. She had no idea what Saint Uwell's was. I'd already been on the Internet, had already done some digging, had already found out that Saint Uwell's was a nice, very expensive nuthouse. I sat there eating my pancakes with real maple syrup, convinced Zanny had no idea was Saint Uwell's was.

Now I wasn't so sure.

Had she thought, even then, I was crazy?

By the time I left the mall, after I'd decided how I could tell Zanny I loved her, I had a plan. Five hours later I was at the computer.

> ~~Did you know you had a secret admirer? Someone~~
> ~~who genuinely appreciates your wit and your~~
> ~~intelligences and your sense of—~~

Oh, my God, I deleted it before I could even look at it.

What could I say, though? What can you say in an anonymous e-mail to an teenage girl that isn't going to completely freak her out? I stared at the sliding doors out to the deck; the family room was dark so I could see through the glass to the moonlit shadows in the back yard. All I could hear was the hum of the computer in front of me.

> ~~I don't know what to say, exactly, about you, that~~
> ~~wouldn't scare you~~
> ~~or make you look over your shoulder every time you~~
> ~~left your house.~~

I had the feeling I was getting further away from what I wanted to say.

~~Hey, Zanny, ever been stalked?~~

I rubbed my eyes, looked at the little clock in the bottom right-hand corner of the monitor. 3:17. I was never up this late. Never. I could have been doing this two hours ago, but Dad and Robin were all over me the second I got home, and they wouldn't let up. Where had I been? Who was I with? What did I think I was doing, hanging up on Robin? It was eleven o'clock at night, and they sat me down at the kitchen table and decided to psychoanalyze me. Blah, blah, blah, blah, we know it's hard, with Mom gone, blah, blah, blah.

"Dad, it's not like it's been months," I pointed out. "Mom left yesterday." A dumb thing to say. Whose side was I on? When an adult gives you an excuse for why you're screwing up, you don't tell him he's stupid.

"Don't you care?" Robin asked, and I had almost a déjà vu feeling because I could vividly remember when Jake and I were five or six and Robin dragged us all over the mall looking for a Christmas present for Mom, asking us the same question, "Don't you care?" Squeezing our little hands and pulling us along, Jake sticking his other hand in his pocket like he didn't mind being dragged around like a rag doll.

"Do you just not care?" Robin asked, again, maybe thinking I didn't understand her the first time. Did she think I was actually going to answer this question?

I looked at Dad. "Is it OK if I get something to eat?"

Dad looked at me like I'd thrown a brick through the window.

"What? I can't eat?"

The interrogation went on until midnight. Then Dad and Robin had their own little conference, whispering in the kitchen. Luckily I was able to use my time wisely, logging onto Netmail and trying to find out if I could send a completely anonymous e-mail and also seeing if I could change the time sent on an e-mail. Turned out you can't do either, or I couldn't figure out how to, anyway, so I set up an e-mail account for John Kurtz of Senegal, Africa. And I logged out and went up to my room and waited.

See, I had a decent criminal mind. I'd seen enough television to know that in order to commit the perfect crime, you had to avoid being a suspect. Suspects always made mistakes, always forgot to act surprised or ask questions anybody would ask. If you were a suspect, you were a goner. And before Zanny even finished reading the e-mail, she was going to be thinking about suspects. She was going to be thinking about who sent it. She'd even write down a list of who it could be.

The only way I'd get away with this was if I wasn't on that list. And since Zanny knew I never, ever stayed up late, if the e-mail was sent in the middle of the night, it would never even occur to her that it could be me.

I just never counted on having to wait until three o'clock in the freaking morning before everyone would go to sleep. Now I could barely keep my eyes open, much less think straight.

~~Oh, Suzannah, don't you cry for me.~~

I dropped my head down and rested it against the edge of the table. Falling asleep was not a good idea, but maybe if I just closed my eyes a second. What did I want to say? What was I trying to tell her? I felt myself falling backward, lifting and swirling. I loved her. Sure, sure, that was it, I thought, coming to rest against a warm, soft blanket.

Whoa. I sat up and shook my head. Then typed.

~~Hey, Suzannah, someone out there loves you. Me.~~

I clicked send without reading it, then grabbed the sides of the keyboard.

"Oh, shit."

It was gone. It was gone, and there was nothing I could do about it. Luckily, I was too tired to sustain any serious panic about it. I turned off the computer and walked slowly through the dark and tip-toed up the stairs. Maybe it was just being so sleepy, but I really took my time on the stairs because Mom heard everything, and it wasn't until I got to the top of the stairs that I remembered Mom wasn't there. I grabbed the handrail. I was tired, too tired, and my eyes filled at the thought of Mom never coming back.

I walked like an old man the rest of the way to my room, where I set the alarm because, of course, I still needed to wake up early, like I always did, and I couldn't let anybody see me yawning, either. As long as I just acted like good ol' Jimmy, I'd be safe.

Bed felt so soft and kind. I pushed my head into my pillow, glad I'd said it. It was out there, somewhere out there in cyberspace. A cyber-dewdrop on a cyber-flower.

Someone out there loves you.

Those words were being stored on a computer in Indianapolis or Des Moines or Ann Arbor, words that absolutely no one knew existed. And tomorrow, sometime, Suzannah would wake up and have some of her grapefruit juice and eventually wander over to the computer. And those words, those very words that had spent the night quietly inside some machine somewhere, would fire their way toward her screen.

And Suzannah would read that someone out there loved her.

I couldn't wait. I had no idea when she'd read it. But I couldn't wait. I went to sleep imagining her eyes reading those words, and I woke up before the alarm went off, thinking about those same words.

The second worst day of my life started with me looking out the window at bare branches knocking around in the wind, wondering if those words were really such a good idea. It sounded a little freaky, I realized now in the bright winter sunshine, this guy declaring his love. It seemed fine at three o'clock in the morning, but after half a night's sleep, it seemed a little over the edge.

Robin was making pancakes when I got downstairs, and she used the white plastic spatula to point to a printout on the kitchen table of an e-mail that Mom had sent in the middle of the night. I stood there with my hands in my pockets and looked down, reading the thing. It said all the stuff you'd expect from a mother who had run away from home. She loved us, this had nothing to do with us, blah blah blah blah.

"There any syrup?" I asked Robin.

She was at the stove and turned to look at me with her mouth open, holding the spatula up in the air like a magic fairy wand. "Mom pours her heart and soul out to you, and all you can ask is, where's the syrup?"

I ignored this, just opened the refrigerator and found the syrup.

"She's suffering, James."

I got out a plate and grabbed three pancakes.

"Your mother is hurting."

"What are these, whole wheat?" I asked, picking up one of the pancakes off my plate and turning it over.

"I understand it hurts, Mom leaving, but what do you think gives you the right to judge her when you have absolutely no idea what's been going on?"

This was so Robin—no one should ever be judged by what they do. In college, she and a bunch of her radical friends had driven all the way to Texas to protest in support of a guy who shot his wife. Just the kind of person I'd want to spend twenty-five hours in the car for.

"OK, Robin," I said, standing there holding my plate in one hand and the syrup in the other. "Why did Mom run away?"

Robin pushed at the edge of a pancake in the pan. "Ask Dad, if you really want to know."

Bluff. She was bluffing. Robin hated admitting when she didn't know what the hell she was talking about.

The doorbell rang.

Mom. Of course I thought it was Mom. Who else would show up at eight o'clock on a Sunday morning?

"Oh, Jesus," Robin said, her voice soft with concern. I looked at her and realized that it wasn't going to be Mom, that when the doorbell rang at eight o'clock on a Sunday morning, it was only going to be bad news. Robin knew that, too. The difference between me and Robin, though, was that she headed for the door while I stood there, not moving, in no rush to know.

I held my breath.

"Zanny?" Robin said, sounding relieved and joyful and confused.

The pancakes really did almost fall off my plate. Damn. I looked over my shoulder, but knew the very worst thing I could do was make a run for it. Running would be admitting everything, would be like handing a signed confession, yes, I sent the e-mail. What I needed to do was stand there and deny, deny, deny.

"Is Jim up?" Zanny asked Robin.

I swallowed hard.

"He's in the kitchen," Robin said. "Come on in."

I hurried to the counter and put the plate and syrup down. Natural, act natural. I reached for the syrup and squeezed some out of the plastic bottle onto the pancakes. Zanny walked right to me.

"We need to talk," she said.

"About what?" I asked, in just the right confused tone. I could do this.

She looked down at my pancakes. "How much syrup do you need?"

I looked at the flood of syrup climbing up the edges of the plate.

"Can we talk in the family room?" Zanny asked.

"I guess. Yeah." I was blowing it, I could feel myself blowing it, and I took deep breaths, like a prizefighter headed into the ring, as I followed Zanny into the family room. Robin had already turned the lights on the Christmas tree, but everything still seemed kind of bare. Mom used to put tons of decorations all over the house—a Christmas train on the round table in the living room, needlepoint Christmas scenes on the walls, a set of Christmas mice on the window sill—so just having the tree now didn't feel all that festive.

Zanny marched to the center of the room and turned around and faced me. "I got an e-mail last night."

My heart stopped, but I didn't miss a beat. I shrugged. "About what?" I asked. I could feel a part of me step out of myself, like a ghost in a movie, and stand there smiling at the two of us. So she knows. So she figured it out.

"Actually, I got two e-mails last night," she said, too wrapped up in what she had to say to pay any attention to the oddness of my smile. Because it wasn't just the ghost that was smiling, I realized. I was smiling. Grinning like an idiot.

"About what?" I asked, again, ready to burst out laughing.

"We need to find your mom."

"We what?"

"Jake sent me a copy of the e-mail she sent you guys. It sounds like she's not very far away. She might even be staying with one of her friends. I bet if we just go around to them, we'll find her car. Then we just hang out and wait for her to come out."

The ghost was gone. "What—? Why—? What is Jake doing, sending you stuff about Mom?"

"What do you mean?" Zanny tossed a hand. "Jake and I e-mail, you know that."

"What?"

"Remember? He sent me that pig poem?"

"The pig poem?" I asked. "Didn't he write that in June? Are you telling me you guys have been e-mailing since June?" I was blowing it. I was really blowing it here.

"On and off, yeah," Zanny said, shrugging. "Look, we'll have plenty of time to talk about all this when we go wait for your mom."

I started shaking my head, trying not to sound as pissed off as I felt. "Why do I need to go find my mother?"

"Because Jake really really needs her."

"Look, Suzannah—"

"He's seeing things," Zanny said, with a finality in her voice like that should be the end of the argument. "He told me in the e-mail last night."

I stuck my hands in my pockets. "What is he seeing?"

"People," she said. "He sees people. He thinks there's someone behind him, and he'll look over his shoulder and he'll think the hat on his coat rack is someone standing there. Or the sheets and blankets sit in a clump and look like someone's lying there."

"So? So tell him to move the coat rack. Tell him to make his bed!"

"There's more," Zanny said.

"What. What more?"

"Just something that tells you how mixed up he is."

"What are you talking about?"

She shook her head. "I don't want to talk about it."

I stared. "You came here to tell me you don't want to tell me something?"

She sighed, closing her eyes. "The other e-mail," she said. "Jake thinks he's in love with me."

Eight

Of course all this gets ignored in *Love Doesn't Grow on Trees*. Zanny never mentions that she thought the e-mail was from Jake. His name doesn't even come up. So of course nobody in America knows that Zanny's obsession with finding Mom had nothing to do with me and everything to do with Zanny's obsession with Jake.

Naturally, all this stuff is off message.

My brother Jake, for instance. My whole twin brother is off message.

At first, I was OK with it. I was OK with not talking about Jake, with Jake not being in Zanny's book. I didn't miss him. It was a relief, really, not having to get into it, just being able to keep the story simple. Me and Zanny, that's all we needed to talk about. It was easy. Nice. Fun.

But when we got to Cleveland on the tour and I finally started writing my book, I realized I couldn't say anything without mentioning Jake. There was no way to tell our story without Jake. If I never mentioned him, I'd be doing more than simplifying the story.

I'd be lying.

I started asking Zanny about it. How could she think it wasn't lying, not mentioning Jake? Weren't we misleading people? Weren't we being dishonest?

At first Zanny just laughed about it, told me I was making way too big a deal out of the whole thing. After a while, though, it got on her nerves, me asking her about Jake, and she decided she wouldn't even talk about him. On our flight last week to Chicago, I brought up

Jake again and Zanny ignored me. Like I wasn't even there, she just reached over, grabbed the air phone, punched in numbers, and then started talking.

"Who is it?" I asked.

Instead of answering, Zanny just handed the phone to me.

It was Mr. Nelson.

"Look, kid, don't be dumb," he told me, over the roar of the plane engines. "You think anybody wants to hear about your brother? You think—" Mr. Nelson choked on the words, like I was strangling him with all this stupidity.

"Kid. We're telling a story," he said, finally. "A story about you and Zanny. Simple. Jake is not part of the story."

I pressed my head back into the seat cushion. "Even if she's in love with him?"

"Will you—?" Mr. Nelson started coughing, hacking like he needed to be hospitalized. "Kid, come on. You know better than that. You never say something like that out loud."

"What. I just asked a question."

"Don't you understand anything? Asking the question makes it true. That's the way it works. Ask that question in front of someone from *People,* and you can't just pack up and go home, it's over."

"But—"

"Look, kid, there's no point in the two of us arguing about it. What do we know, right? This is what you do. You just concentrate on writing your little book—" This was two days before Minneapolis; Mr. Nelson was still being pushy about the book. "You get your little book done, you send it off to me, and we'll have the editors look things over, OK? They're the experts, they're the professionals. We'll let them decide what to include. OK? How's that sound?"

Zanny was coming back from the bathroom, sitting down, not looking at me. "Sure," I said. "OK, Mr. Nelson."

And when I got off the phone, I made sure not to mention Jake again.

Or let Zanny see what I was typing into my laptop.

Because I didn't care what anybody said, I was going to tell the world that Zanny thought Jake was John Kurtz from Senegal, Africa. I wanted the world to know that Zanny thought Jake was the one in love with her.

I stood there in the family room that Mom hadn't decorated for Christmas, blinking at Zanny.

"So Jake thinks he's love with you. So what?" It bugged me that Zanny had immediately decided it was Jake who sent the stupid e-mail, but what I needed to find out now was what she planned on doing about it.

"So what? Are you kidding?" Zanny rolled her eyes. "He's as bad as your character in the play."

I didn't get it. "Why? Did he call you Zanny, goddess, nymph, perfect, divine?"

"He said he's in love with me. That's weird enough."

"What's weird about it?"

"This is Jake we're talking about," Zanny said. "Jake is not an idiot."

I didn't say anything. Just stood there blinking.

Zanny made a circle motion with her hand. "Are you coming with me or not?"

Of course I was going with her. I was madly in love with her. I was an idiot. I wasn't about to turn down the chance to be with her.

We went out and got in Zanny's car. I sat there with my arms crossed.

"We're just going to drive around looking for Mom's car?" I asked, watching Zanny turn right on Main Street. "Wouldn't it be a lot easier to call her?"

Zanny looked at me. "You didn't read the e-mail your mom sent everyone?"

"You're telling me Jake actually sent it to you?"

"You're avoiding the question."

"Was this before or after declaring his love to you? O fairest Zanny."

Zanny sighed. "Your mom turned off her cell. She's intentionally not checking her own e-mail. She said she loves the three of you more than anything on earth, but she just needs a few days alone to sort things out."

I shook my head. "Then why are we hunting her down?"

"Because this is an emergency," Zanny said, without hesitation. "She needs to know how close to the edge Jake is."

"What are you talking about? Jake is always close to the edge. He brags about being close to the edge."

"You don't have to come with me," Zanny said. "Just give me the names and addresses. I'll go alone."

We found Mom's car in less than an hour, parked in Stormy Tidewater's driveway. Stormy was divorced but didn't have to work because her ex-husband had made millions bankrupting a company that made cheap party favors. Stormy lived in a huge colonial in the historic district. The street was beautiful, even with the trees bare and exposing an ashy-gray sky. Zanny drove around the block and came down the street again and parked two houses down.

Five hours later we were still there, and we had no idea if anyone was even home. We'd gone over Zanny's lines, we'd gone over my lines, we'd played a couple of hundred games of twenty questions. And I'd sat there in the cold with my arms crossed and started thinking that Mom and Dad might really get divorced.

Divorced. It just didn't seem possible. How could anyone who knew Mom and Dad think it was possible?

"Zanny, I'm starving here," I said, squeezing my ribs with my arms.

"I told you, let's order pizza," she said, reading *The Castle*, a Kafka book about a guy going to a castle who never even actually gets there.

"You can't honestly believe a pizza place is going to deliver to a car," I told her, desperate to get out of there. "Let's just go down to the Exxon station, I can grab some chips. It'll take three seconds."

"And what if your mother just happens to come out in those three seconds?"

"We're not getting paid for this, you know. We're not professionals."

My cell chimed in with *Jingle Bells.*

I imagined Mom inside the house, looking through the curtains at Zanny's car, calling me, asking me to leave. Instead it was Gene, asking if I knew where Mary was. He couldn't reach her on her cell, and she always had it on. He didn't understand why she wouldn't take his call.

I collapsed against the seat. Oh, God. With everything going on with Mom and Zanny, I'd been able to completely forget what a jerk I'd been to Gene. He hadn't just disappeared, though, and I knew now was the time to tell him the truth, now was the time to tell him that Mary, that his girlfriend, had stayed out late at Sam's Pizza with a guy from Connecticut.

"I don't know," I said, instead. "You want to talk to Zanny?"

"You suck," Zanny told me, taking the phone, knowing this was not a conversation she was going to want to have. "Gene? Hi. What's wrong? Mary's not answering her cell? Really. You're kidding me. Really?"

Zanny raised her hand up between us and gave me the finger.

"No, no, I have no idea. Maybe her phone isn't charged?"

Zanny was brilliant at lying. It made me wonder, sitting there next to her, how many times she had lied to me. When we were friends, I didn't care, it didn't matter, people lied, so what? But now. Now it made a difference. Now if she lied to me and I believed it, then who did I love? Did I love Zanny? Or did I love this idea of Zanny based on the lies she'd told me?

I looked out my window. I knew I wouldn't be thinking this way if I hadn't been stuck in this freaking car for five hours, wanting to just reach over and throw my arms around this girl, but it was a little scary to think about who Zanny was. To think about how she'd treated Mark Noonan, refusing to kiss him because he was a Republican. Or Henry Poplar, letting him touch her breast on the outside of her shirt but then asking him if he thought he was picking a grapefruit at the grocery store. Or this, this right here, sitting in this car for hours and hours so she can talk to my mother and save Jake.

This whole Jake thing. The e-mails going back and forth between her and Jake for months. Months!

E-mails she never talked about, never mentioned. That was not a good sign. Zanny and I e-mailed every day and talked about everything; I thought I was as inside her life as anyone could get. Now I found out there was another layer, further inside, and my twin brother was hanging out in there with her.

Zanny got off the phone with Gene and I kept looking outside my window.

"So how often do you guys e-mail?"

"Are you talking about Jake?"

I felt a fist clenching inside my stomach. "He forwards e-mails from my mother to you?"

"He knew I was concerned about you guys."

My backpack was sitting there between us, and I reached in and pulled out my script for *A Midsummer Night's Dream*.

"Are you trying to tell me you're jealous?" Zanny asked.

"I'm telling you it seems kind of weird, him sending you e-mails from my mother."

"Maybe that's because you won't even talk about her. Not a single word. You don't think that's weird?"

"What. You already know everything."

"Look, asshole," Zanny said, shaking her head, "Jake thought she sounded sad in the e-mail, but he couldn't figure out why, and he was asking me if I could see what it was about the message that seemed so sad."

"A mother abandons her family and Jake can't figure out what's sad about it?"

Zanny and I glared at each other. She wanted to talk about Jake, fine, we'd talk about Jake.

"Let's just get some food," Zanny said, annoyed, changing the subject. She called Gene back and asked him to pick up some burgers and bring them over. Gene thought it was cool that we were on this stake-out, and he told Zanny he'd be right over.

"We should tell him," I said, when Zanny hung up.

"Tell him what?"

"Tell him about the Connecticut boy wonder."

Zanny lifted her palms up, her mouth open. I braced myself, knew this was going to be bad. "We should tell him? Am I his best friend? Am I the one who made him think Mary was buying him an incredibly wonderful present? Am I the one who lied so I could go spy on my friend's girlfriend?"

Jingle Bells. My phone was going off again.

Zanny pointed at the phone. "You're the one who needs to tell Gene and you know it."

"What," I said, into the phone.

"Jake?"

I pulled the phone away from my head and looked at it. "Janine?"

Zanny looked over. "Janine?"

"Goddamn," Janine said, "you sound just like your brother."

Janine was Jake's girlfriend.

"Why's she calling you?" Zanny asked.

I shrugged. "How're you doing?" I asked into the phone. "What, uh—What's up?"

"Smooth," Zanny said.

Janine was only seventeen, but she'd dropped out of school and was living on her own, so she seemed older. I'd seen her at a couple of parties where she was drunk and laughing her ass off, but I'd never actually said more than "let me get him" to her.

"Hey, Jake isn't there with you, by any chance, is he?" she asked.

"No, but I've got his number," I told her.

"Yeah, so do I," she said. "But you're the one I want to talk to."

"Oh."

Zanny saw my eyes widen. "What's wrong?" she asked.

Janine cleared her throat. "Listen, I know this is stupid to be doing this, but I wanted to ask you about that friend of yours, Suzie Zoony Something. The one with the hair?"

"Uh-huh," I said, switching the phone to my other ear.

"What, what?" Zanny asked, practically panting. If something was going on, she had to know about it. She always claimed she was just looking for a good story that she could write, but she also loved knowing everything about everyone. Maybe even my mom. Was that part of the reason we were sitting here in the car? So Zanny could find out what was up with Mom?

"What's up with her?" Janine asked.

"I—I don't know. What—like—what do you mean?"

"What does she want?" Zanny whispered, forward, smiling. "Ask her what she wants."

"Are you and Suzie a thing?" Janine asked.

"I—no," I told her.

"Come on, come on," Zanny said, hurrying me along with her hands. "What's she trying to find out?"

Janine said something, too, but I didn't catch it. "What?" I asked, plugging up my ear next to Zanny.

"I know this sounds juvenile," Janine said, quickly, "but I'm trying to find out if your little friend it trying to steal my fucking boyfriend."

"I—uhh—I—"

Zanny slapped my arm. "What is she asking?" she whispered, desperately. I wanted to shout at her.

"Best guess," Janine asked, "what would you say?"

"Uhh—" I just wanted to get this over with, and I hated Zanny for how interested she was in this conversation, how she started drooling and fidgeting as soon as she heard it was Janine. "Maybe," I said.

"Shit."

"Maybe what? Maybe what?" Zanny asked.

"I have no idea!" I told Janine, trying to cover up my mistake.

"About what?" Zanny asked. "What do you have no idea about?"

"I need to go," I said, ready to explode.

"Ask her why she wants to know," Zanny said.

"Jake thinks she's a goddamn genius, the way he talks about her," Janine said. "Is she a goddamn genius?"

"I doubt it," I said. "I'll see you." I hit the red button on the phone before more words came out of it.

"What the hell was that about?"

I stared through the windshield. A goddamn genius. Jake thought Zanny was a goddamn genius. And she thought Jake was a goddamn genius.

"What's wrong?" Zanny asked, watching me. "Jimmy? What's going on?" Her voice was softer, anxious. "Is Jake OK?"

I didn't blink.

"Jim."

"He's fine," I said, checking the rearview mirror and seeing a car pull up behind us. "Gene's here."

"Jim. Talk to me," Zanny said.

"I want to eat," I said.

Zanny studied me. "I don't understand."

"Me, either," I said, and Gene climbed into the backseat and the car filled with the aroma of burgers and fries and Gene started having a fit because he'd asked the guy at Burger King to put things into three different bags, one for Zanny, one for me, and one for Gene, but instead everything was thrown together into one bag. Not only that, but all the fries were now in a heap at the bottom of the bag. While Gene hyperventilated, trying to sort out the fries, Zanny looked at me suspiciously.

"A Tufts alum lives a block down," Gene said, handing out burgers.

We both looked over our shoulders at him.

"Class of '82," Gene said. "He goes to the same church Mary does."

"Gene," Zanny said. "This Tufts thing is getting a little freaky."

"Hey, it's called networking," Gene said. "Don't you guys read any of the books? Do you have any idea how many applications Tufts is getting this year?"

I put my burger down. This was like that peasant painting Jake was talking about, where the peasants are completely clueless about Icarus crashing into the water. Here was my best friend going on and on about Tufts when he should be moaning about losing his girlfriend to some guy from Connecticut.

Grandma would have been proud of the guilt I felt.

"Gene," I said, knowing I needed to do the right thing.

"Who's that?" Zanny asked.

A shiny blue Volvo was pulling up in front of Stormy Tidewater's house.

"That's the new 427," Gene said. "It just came out."

"What is he talking about?" Zanny asked.

"The car," I told her, as all of us watched a tall guy unfold himself from the car.

"Oh, my God," Zanny asked.

"Is he the husband?" Gene asked.

"The husband lives in Michigan," I told him, watching the guy open up the back seat and reach inside.

"What does this Stormy Tidewater look like?" Zanny asked.

"Okay," I said, still watching the guy. He was taking forever, whatever he was doing.

"Maybe he's a repairman," she said.

Gene snorted. "That's a forty-seven-thousand-dollar car."

"OK, guys, could we shut up?"

The guy pulled a tree, an enormous potted palm tree, out of the backseat.

"Oh, my God," Zanny said.

"That's a sugar palm," Gene said.

"Will you please?" I asked. I grabbed the steering wheel and watched the guy walk up to the front door. He rang the bell and put the plant down and I could feel my heart working as I looked at the Christmas tree in the house next door. It was late and the sky was turning dark.

My mom opened the door and stepped outside and changed my life.

Nine

I wasn't crushed, though. It wasn't the devastating experience that Zanny makes it sound like in *Love Doesn't Grow on Trees*. She even talks about "tears welling up in his eyes." Which would kind of make sense, if I was the nice, dumb kid that the world is supposed to think I am. If a nice kid sees his mother kissing some strange guy, chances are the kid is going to want to cry.

I'm not the nice kid, though. Crying never even occurred to me. At first, I was just stunned. It seemed like I wasn't seeing right. I sat there remembering back in the third grade, when some bald mad scientist guy came into our classroom and told us that our eyes actually see everything upside down, and that our brains turn everything right side up so it makes sense. Seeing Mom kiss the tall man with the palm tree was so hard to believe, so spectacularly unbelievable, it was like my brain wasn't working, wasn't making the right conversion, wasn't turning everything rightside up.

After the shock wore off, though, I was way too pissed off to even think about crying. So Mom was having an affair with some tall guy with a palm tree. What the hell was there to cry about?

The three of us sat there and watched the tall man let go of my mom and pick up the palm tree and follow her inside. For a second no one said anything, like we'd been in a car crash and were too dazed to speak.

"Who—?" Gene started, but Zanny spun around on him and he shut up.

"We're going to go now," she said, glaring at Gene, who was all for leaving and wasted no time getting out of the car. Zanny drove back to my house without saying a word and just let me go inside without trying to get me to talk about it. Talking about it was something phenomenally overrated. Why? For what? What was there to talk about?

Robin was in the kitchen, making oatmeal chocolate chip cookies that would have too much oatmeal and not enough chocolate chips because Robin couldn't resist trying to make even cookies healthy. I walked through the kitchen without stopping but then got to the family room and saw the back of Dad's head. He was watching the Giants on TV. I stood there, perfectly still, looking at Dad's little balding spot that was so far back on his head that I wondered if he even knew it was there. Did Dad know we could see all the way through to his scalp? Did he know his hair was grayer and thinner where he couldn't see it?

What exactly did he know about what was going on behind his back?

The Giants were close, but as I was standing there the Eagles ran the ball up the middle for eight or nine yards, and I could just tell the Giants would not be making a comeback. I looked over at the sliding glass doors. The backyard was dark already, and the room was reflected in the glass. When would he find out, I wondered. When would Mom tell Dad about the tall man? After Christmas, I hoped. Or after New Year's. Or never. Never would be good.

Slant pattern across the middle, missed tackle, touchdown Eagles.

"Hmm," Dad said. "That's not good."

He needed to know. Dad needed to know about the tall man with the palm tree. I would have wanted to know. It stopped you from making a complete idiot out of yourself, knowing. I was glad I knew about Zanny, glad I knew how she felt about Jake. I got embarrassed just thinking about what I might have ended up saying to her, if I hadn't known.

I turned and stared at the computer and wondered what Zanny had said to Kurtz. She was so sure it was Jake, what did she say to him? When I'd been with her back in the car, I'd decided Kurtz was dead, I was going to log in and delete the guy, wipe him off the face of the earth.

Now, though, I wondered what she said to him. What did she tell him? Did it matter to her at all that Jake was already seeing someone?

I was glad, now, that Janine had called, that Zanny was reminded that Jake had a girlfriend. Did Zanny know Janine had her own apartment? Did she know Jake practically lived there sometimes? Did it matter to Zanny that this guy she was so crazy about was already taken? Or was it like the play, where people just loved people for no good reason?

I looked back at Dad. Did it matter to the tall man with the palm tree that Mom was married? Did it matter to him that in college Dad had stayed up all night wrapped in a blanket in the cold because he loved Mom so much? Did it matter to him that he was destroying a family?

I walked over and sat down at the computer and logged in as Kurtz. He had three messages: one claiming he was a hot stud, one suggesting he increase the size of his penis, and one from Zanny:

> From: suzannah007@netmail.com
> To: kurtz4now@netmail.com
> Date: 5 December 8:16 am
> Subject: What do YOU know about it?
>
> What could you possibly know about love? And for that matter, what could you possibly know about me?

I read it twice and decided to write back.

> From: kurtz4now@netmail.com
> To: suzannah007@netmail.com
> Date: 5 December 5:19 pm
> Subject: Arrogance
>
> You think you and love are really so complicated and mysterious?

Robin was in a chatty mood at dinner and acted like we were just one big happy family. Dad and Jake went along with it, the three of them remembering a cold and rainy camping trip when Dad got a fishing hook stuck in his thumb and all of us pleaded to go with him to the emergency room because it would be warm and dry.

"Mom cried about her sweater getting singed in the campfire," I said, standing up and bringing my plate over to the sink, glad to hear the laughing die down over at the table.

"The blue one with the gold threads," Dad called over to me. "She bought it when she was pregnant with Robin."

He was being nostalgic about one of Mom's freaking sweaters. What was wrong with him? Was he still in love with her? Was Dad really still in love with her? It made my stomach sink, thinking about Dad still being in love with Mom when she and her boyfriend were inside Stormy Tidewater's house doing who knew what. I scraped my plate off, wanting to tell him, wanting to just shout at all three of them about the tall man with the palm tree. Instead I shoved my plate into the dishwasher and went upstairs and turned my boom box up loud. I tried working on my lines for the play, but I just sat there on the bed holding my script and thinking about Zanny and thinking about Mom and thinking about how I could shake this hollowed-out feeling inside.

Someone pounded on my door loud enough to be heard over the music. Dad telling me to turn it down, probably.

"WHAT," I hollered through the door.

Jake opened the door and stood there, blinking. His hair was a wreck, and I didn't know if it was that or the jeans torn wide open at both knees, but for some reason he looked more Jesus-like than usual.

I still had no patience for him. "What."

He walked closer and I could see the little stoned grin. Was he stoned? It was impossible to tell for sure anymore. Jake pointed at my boom box and shouted, "I turn the radio up loud, so I don't have to think."

Springsteen. He was quoting Springsteen. He didn't even like Springsteen. Dad liked Springsteen. Jake mostly liked people who ended up killing themselves.

I reached over and turned it down. "Something you want to talk about?"

He nodded slowly. "E-mail."

My heart lurched. E-mail? I grabbed my copy of *A Midsummer Night's Dream* and opened it up. "What about it?"

"I've been talking to Mom," he said.

"You wrote her?"

"She's here in town."

"At Stormy Tidewater's house," I told him, trying not to show how much I enjoyed seeing his surprise.

"How did you find out?" he asked. "Did you follow her?"

"Did you write to her?" I asked back. "Even though she didn't want us e-mailing?"

Jake smiled. "You followed her. That's so cool."

Yeah, cool. Up until I saw her make out with the tall man with the palm tree. That wasn't so cool.

I looked down at my script, couldn't deal with Jake being a human being for once. What was going on? What was he after?

"She wants to see us," he said.

"No, thanks."

"She just wants to talk."

"Tell her I say hi," I said, still staring at my script. Jake just stood there, waiting for me to look up at him, but that wasn't about to happen.

"Robin and I have been talking to her," Jake said, finally. "There's more to it than you know."

"Oh, yeah," I agreed, my hands holding tight to the script, ready to tear it apart. More to it? There was more to it, all right. There was a bunch more to it, a whole mountain more to it. It was great finding out just how much more.

When I got to rehearsal after school the next day, Bertram Diller was down at the foot of the stage getting his horse head adjusted by Ms. Farling, who always did the costumes and scenery for Mr. Fricker. In the play, Bertram's character, Bottom, ticks off some fairies, so they turn him into a jackass. Ms. Farling was making sure the horse head was on tight so Bertram could do his dance with Sheila Murphy, who was playing Titania, queen of the fairies. Titania falls in love with the jackass because of a magic potion another fairy squirts in her eyes when she's asleep.

That's Shakespeare for you.

Ms. Farling reached inside the horse's head and gave a couple of tugs and told Bertram to try it out. Bertram and Sheila were both incredible dancers, so I walked down next to Zanny and watched Bertram, wearing this enormous horse's head, doing all these fancy steps and spinning Sheila around. People actually applauded when they were done.

"Next!" Bertram called out, his horse head turning from side to side as he looked for another partner. He reached out and grabbed Ms. Farling's hand. She laughed and let him lead her around for a while until Bertram spun her so hard toward those of us watching that Ms. Farling almost went flying right into me. We were nose to nose, and I guessed it scared Ms. Farling, how we could have smashed heads. She just stared at me and stopped and pulled her hand away from Bertram.

"Sorry," she said, her eyes darting as she straightened her hair and walked away.

"Hmmm," Zanny said.

I looked at her. She was watching Ms. Farling walk away. "What?"

"Did you see that?" Zanny asked, not taking her eyes off Ms. Farling.

"See what?"

"How guilty she looked."

"What are you talking about?"

Zanny kept staring at Ms. Farling, eyes narrowed. "They're having sex."

"Who?"

Zanny's eyes went to Bertram.

"Ms. Farling and—" Bertram? Give me a break. Zanny thought Ms. Farling would have sex with Cape Boy? "They're not having sex, Zanny."

"Then what does she feel so guilty about?"

"She's not—They're not—" I was spluttering. It totally sucked that Zanny would accuse Ms. Farling of having an affair with Bertram Diller. She was probably going to start writing about this supposed affair in her little journal book.

"PEOPLE," Mr. Fricker called.

"OK, people," Beverly Tungsten, our stage manager, called out. "Let's gather."

By now everyone knew that Mr. Fricker shouting "people" meant hop up on stage and sit in a big circle with Fricker standing there in the center. He stood there and waited until we were pin-drop silent.

"LOVE IS ETERNAL!" he bellowed, turning slowly, meeting our eyes. "We like to think. We want to believe. In another of Shakespeare's plays, Romeo and Juliet die for each other's love. Isn't that nice? Isn't that sweet? But what happened to poor old—?" Fricker snapped his fingers a couple of times. "What's her name again? The woman, the young girl Romeo happened to be IN LOVE WITH AT THE BEGINNING OF THE PLAY? We have the greatest love story in the history of literature, and the boy STARTS OUT IN LOVE WITH SOMEONE ELSE."

Mr. Fricker swung his arm around violently and then stopped to take a deep breath. "Why? Why does Shakespeare do this to us? Why in our *Midsummer Night's Dream* do we have couples running around in the forest falling in and out of love and a queen waxing romantic over a man who's been turned into a jackass?" Mr. Fricker looked around as if actually looking for an answer, but no one was dumb enough to raise a hand, or even move. "Because love is absurd. Love is foolish. Love is dumb. And transient, unfathomably transient. It evaporates, disappears."

I glanced over at Zanny and saw her staring down at the floor.

"Mind you, Shakespeare tells us, love is also intensely wonderful, perhaps the most wonderful feeling on earth, so you'd better damn well 'gather ye rosebuds while ye may.' BECAUSE IT'S NOT GOING TO BE AROUND FOR LONG. Don't be an idiot and squander it or stifle it, not for your family, not for your country, not for anything should you seal your heart off from the greatest joy of your life."

I sat there, my head turned, keeping my eyes away from Zanny, not wanting to see her glazed eyes, not wanting to know who she was thinking about.

No one was there when I got home, and I sat at the kitchen table and tried doing the calculus homework, but Mr. Fricker's words haunted me. "Don't be an idiot and squander it or stifle it."

I stood up. I tried pushups, tried splashing cold water on my face, and then I gave up and went into the family room and logged on as Kurtz. Just out of curiosity. Just to see if Zanny had written back.

I saw her name in the in-box and could feel my heart beating. I looked over my shoulder and listened to make sure Jake hadn't gotten home before I opened up the message.

From: suzannah007@netmail.com
To: kurtz4now@netmail.com
Date: 6 December 5:12 pm
Subject: Here's the deal

Delete this message, read it, delete it, make it
disappear, I promise to do the same to your messages,
just so we know, this is temporary, this is an in-the-
meantime thing, I know this shouldn't be an anything,
we shouldn't be talking, not after you claimed to love
me, and if I believed it, if I didn't trust you to be the
only person I can trust NOT to love me, not the wrong
way, I wouldn't write another word to you, and I will
only say this once, but today I was talked out of giving
you up, maybe Mr. Kurtz you have read The Heart Of
Darkness and maybe you get it the way the rest of
them do not, that it's about us, that darkness isn't
somebody else's jungle, it's the one residing right
here inside you and me, that darkness I will let no one
see not even you so don't ask.

I was out of breath after reading her message, as if I had tried to
read the whole thing out loud in one breath. I sat there for a long time,
not thinking anything, just feeling this click, like the tumblers had
fallen into place. I didn't want to read her note over again and maybe
spoil the magic. I reached for the mouse to log out, to leave it alone,
but couldn't do it.

Don't squander it or stifle it.

Even if it was stupid, even if it wasn't quite real. Even if Zanny got
it completely wrong about who she was talking to.

From: kurtz4now@netmail.com
To: suzannah007@netmail.com
Date: 6 December 5:34 pm
Subject: Dark Heart

When my dad was young, a psychiatrist asked him if,
when he saw the train pulling into the station, he
ever thought of jumping in front of it. And my Dad
laughed and admitted that yeah, he had.
    Are you the train pulling into the station?
    What, I wonder, is inside the heart of Suzannah
Manning that she does not want anyone to know
about.

I logged out quickly, like I was afraid of someone bursting in with a gun and pointing it at me. Was I playing fair? Was I cheating? Zanny thought Kurtz was someone else. Was it wrong to feel connected to someone like that, to feel a warmth in your chest, a life different from anything you'd ever known, when the person you're making that connection with believes she's talking to someone else?

The phone rang.

I jumped away from the portable phone, standing up on the corner of the desk like Grandma's statue of John the Baptist. God, I couldn't believe how guilty I felt, sending off that Kurtz e-mail. Like I was a little kid again, leaving the confessional knowing I'd never mentioned the real sins but ones made up to sound just like what the nuns had suggested in our Wednesday afternoon class.

The phone rang a second time. I took in all the air I could get before grabbing it.

"Hello?"

"We need to have sex."

Ten

The call wasn't for me.

I didn't even recognize the voice, but I knew, whoever it was, she wasn't calling me.

Now, of course, it's different. Now I wouldn't be a bit surprised, some woman calling and saying those five words to me. You get to be a little famous, and it's amazing what happens. First the whole kissing Jim thing, with girls, women trying to kiss me everywhere we went. Then the underwear. I didn't know how it started, but suddenly women were sending me their underwear. Victoria's Secret type stuff. At first just a few pairs, but then somehow *People* magazine heard about it and did a little item and everywhere we went, people started asking us about the underwear.

Of course underwear is not on message. If anybody asked us about the underwear, Mr. Nelson said we were just supposed to act embarrassed and not say anything. Me and Zanny are not about underwear—the entire world knows we've never done it, we're both still virgins. That's a big part of our image, is this virgin purity. Apparently some woman at *The New York Times* wrote an article theorizing that the whole reason the kissing Jim thing and the underwear thing got started in the first place was because of our image of purity—women felt inspired by, attracted to, our virginity.

She was wrong.

A week after the little blurb appeared in *People*, I started getting sacks of underwear. Every time we had an interview the underwear was just about the only thing people asked us about. And I'd have to shrug and try to blush and act like I didn't want to talk about it.

The fact is, though, I thought it was a riot. I mean, women were sending me their underwear. I know a lot of girls are going to think this is weird, but I can't imagine any sixteen year old guy who wouldn't think it was pretty cool. I couldn't stop laughing, sometimes, holding up a pair of underwear and imagining someone actually wearing something that uncomfortable.

What made it even funnier was how it drove Zanny up a wall. The kissing Jim thing she thought was funny. Mr. Nelson explained to us that having these girls and women trying to kiss me all the time was great publicity, and Zanny thought it was a riot, how fidgety I would get in a crowd, looking over my shoulder, worried some woman was going to grab me.

The underwear was different, though. Zanny didn't think the underwear was funny at all. When they first started coming in, I showed her some of the pairs I got, but in Tucson Zanny called me a pervert and wouldn't talk to me all the way to Phoenix. After that I knew enough to not even mention the underwear, but other people brought it up all the time, and Zanny's body would get all tense as soon as anyone said the word. I tried not to look at her because I had a hard time not cracking up, seeing her get all uptight about it.

"You love it," she sneered at me as we left a TV studio in Dallas.

This was the day before we flew to Minneapolis. We'd just been interviewed for a local talk-show, and the guy interviewing us had made a big deal about the underwear, had called me a rock star, a super-hero. The studio audience thought it was a riot, and kept applauding, but Zanny sat there with her arms crossed, looking ready to explode.

"You just love it," she muttered.

That was what drove her crazy, was how much I enjoyed it.

"That fake shrug of yours?"

I tried not to smile. "Fake shrug?"

We were standing by ourselves, waiting for an elevator. "And panties," Zanny said, completely disgusted. "Anytime someone says panties, you turn away, like you're embarrassed, but I can see the lascivious pleasure you get out of it."

"The what?" I couldn't stop the smiling, now, and was trying not to burst out laughing.

"And you think you deserve it," she said.

I was squinting at her, couldn't stop the laughter spilling out. "What are you talking about?"

Zanny looked at me, her mouth flat, hating the laughter, hating my joy. "You think the underwear is about you," she spat.

I stepped back, couldn't believe the sound of her voice.

"The underwear has nothing to do with you," Zanny said, stepping toward me, her anger building, the words getting louder. "The underwear is about Phil Nelson. Phil Nelson is the one who started the underwear. He planned the whole thing. Just like he planned the whole kissing Jim thing. He planned it all, but he didn't want me telling you about it because he was worried you'd be an idiot and blab to the world about it!"

I couldn't move, couldn't breathe. I actually forgot to breathe, and suddenly was gasping for air.

I realized it was Janine on the phone. It was Janine, calling for Jake. I had no idea what to say. "Uh?"

"Oh, shit. Jimmy? Jimmy, is that you?" She started to laugh. "Oh, shit, I'm so sorry. I was sure it was Jake. God, you sounded so much like him."

I still didn't know what to say. Forget about mistaking me for Jake over the phone, which no one had done since we were maybe four. It was what Janine actually said that got to me.

We need to have sex.

That was what she'd said. I'd heard it. "Let me—I'm not—" I pointed to the stairs. "I'll see if Jake's around."

I went to the foot of the stairs and hollered "telephone!" and waited until Jake's door opened before I sat the portable phone on the stairs—either he'd see it and go over to Janine's and have sex or he'd trip over it and die. I let God decide and opened the front door and went out and stood in my socks in the freezing cold. Did girls think that way? When you were going out with a girl and the two of you were actually having sex, did they say things like that? I knew theoretically there had to be girls out there who wanted to have sex, but I couldn't believe there were more than a dozen girls in the state of New Jersey who would call their boyfriend and say it.

The next day at lunch I couldn't shake that "we need to have sex" phone conversation with Janine.

"How much do girls want it?"

Zanny looked up from her notebook. "Is this a multiple-choice question?"

"I'm serious," I told her. "How much do they really want to have sex?"

"Look, Jimmy," she said. "Unless her name's Gigi Walker, I wouldn't be getting my hopes up."

"I'm talking if they really like a guy."

Zanny tilted her head. "Who are you asking about?"

I blinked. "Girls. In general."

"You want me to speak for half the species?"

"Why not?"

"Did I mention I'm a virgin?"

"You're still a girl."

"What are you two talking about now?" Gene complained, still holding the same pickle he'd picked up when he sat down.

It was Tuesday and again, instead of sitting with us, Mary was sitting at table six with Allison Fogel and all the rest of the girls she'd sat with back in freshman year, before she started dating Gene.

"Sex?" Gene asked, annoyed. "Are you talking about sex?"

He'd been staring over at table six without trying to look like he'd been staring over at table six. Without any explanation, Mary had dumped him Monday morning during homeroom. Later Gene had spent lunch looking over at table six like a puppy dog left to starve, and Mary had warned him at play rehearsal to leave her alone or she'd call the police. So now on Tuesday he was pretending to eat the pickle, using it as camouflage.

"Jimmy wants me to tell him how much girls like sex," Zanny told him.

"That's not what I said," I pointed out. "I want to know how much they want sex. I'm just wondering, when they really like someone, do they really want to have sex? Do they get to be like . . . guys?"

"No way," Gene said.

"Excuse me," Zanny said, glaring at Gene and then looking back at me. "No way."

"Then why do they do it?" I asked her. "Why do girls ever have sex?"

Zanny squeezed her eyes shut. "Do you know how pathetic you sound?"

"Why are you a virgin?" I asked.

Zanny's mouth dropped open as she looked around. "Post it on the Internet, why don't you?"

"What. You're embarrassed?"

"Aren't you?"

I watched her for a few seconds. "How come you never answer a question?"

Zanny moved back in her seat, like I'd shoved her.

"You want to know all the gossip," I said, pointing at her journal, "everything about everyone else. You even make up gossip about people—"

"I'm not making anything up. You saw how guilty Ms. Farling looked. There's something going on with her and Bertram, you wait and see."

"—but you never want anybody to know anything about you."

Zanny was smiling at me now. "Not unless they read about in *People*."

Zanny's mouth changed as she watched me watching her.

"What's gotten into you?" she asked, finally.

I didn't say anything. Not until I got on the computer that night.

> From: kurtz4now@netmail.com
> To: suzannah007@netmail.com
> Date: 6 December 19:03 pm
> Subject: Voices

> I can hear you on paper. I can hear your voice when
> you write. I can hear your words, and I can hear
> your smile. I can hear the smell of your shampoo.
> And your shyness, the shyness you try to hide.
> When I see you, you seem less real to me because
> this right here feels like the real thing, the real you.

The next day at lunch, Zanny was on her cell, calling other people in the cafeteria, asking them what they knew about Ms. Farling. What kind of car did she drive, where did she live, what did she buy at the grocery store.

"This is not investigative reporting," I said, pointing to her notebook. "It's gossiping."

"Not if you make money at it," Zanny said.

"You just want to know what's going on," I told her.

Zanny laughed into her notebook. "Everybody wants to know what's going on," she said. "I just want to be the one to tell them."

```
From:     kurtz4now@netmail.com
To:       suzannah007@netmail.com
Date:     15 December 10:43 pm
Subject:  Still life
```

I heard you laugh today, a little embarrassed. It was a frozen moment, like a snapshot, maybe in black and white, slightly blurry, full of motion and sound and slightly off-center.

Writing to her made me want to see her, and seeing her made me want to write. I was living two lives, and they were feeding off each other.

The next day, in English, Ms. Farling started talking about a Joseph Conrad story, "The Secret Sharer," we were supposed to have read. It's about a sea captain who secretly hides a murderer who looks just like him.

"How does it impact our lives, when we hide something?" Ms. Farling asked, in a far away voice. "What does it do to us to secretly share our lives with someone? How does it change us? How do they become a part of us?"

Out of the corner of my eye I could see Zanny trying to get my attention. Eventually, she couldn't take it anymore and reached over and jabbed me with her pencil.

"Oww," I said.

Ms. Farling looked over but her eyes still had a glazed look to them. "What does it do to everyone involved?" she asked.

"What'd I tell you?" Zanny asked, when she showed up at rehearsal. "Didn't I tell you?"

I was in the third row of the auditorium, reading "The Secret Sharer." Ms. Farling was one of those nice teachers who didn't believe in pop quizzes, so no one ever did the reading, but now I wanted to know how it turned out. The captain keeps calling the murderer his double, his other self, and I just slid further and further down into the seat, thinking about the other self I was hiding. Thinking about Kurtz, who could say things that I could never say, who could use words I'd never allow myself to use. I knew people were always pretending to be other people on the Internet—girls pretending they were guys, guys pretending they were over twenty-one. This was different, though. Kurtz wasn't someone else. Kurtz was me. Kurtz was this other self.

"Look! Look, look!" Zanny said, nudging me.

Bertram and Ms. Farling were up on the stage, Bertram pulling himself up into a tree Ms. Farling had built as part of the set.

"So?"

"Do you see the way she pushed her boobs at him?"

"She didn't push anything," I said. "And you told me they were called breasts."

"This is the story," Zanny said.

"What?"

"I'm telling you, this is the one."

"The one that's going to make you famous?"

"It's full of sociological implications," Zanny said, writing furiously in her notebook.

I rolled my eyes and watched her, watched her hair falling across her face. "Why do you like thinking everyone's doing it?"

"I don't think everyone's doing it," Zanny said. "Did I ever accuse Mr. Grout of doing it?"

"How are you going to prove this?" I asked. "How are you going to prove Bertram and Ms. Farling are doing it?"

Zanny slowly turned her head toward me, grinning like some mad scientist ready to take over the world.

Two days later, the doorbell rang. Saturday night, eight o'clock. Mom, I thought. Even knowing about the tall man with the palm tree, for a fraction of a second every time I heard the phone, every time I heard the doorbell, I thought it was Mom coming back. Mom, asking forgiveness.

I opened the door. It was Zanny.

"She ordered Chinese," Zanny said. "For two."

I just stood there, the door still open.

"Ms. Farling," Zanny shouted, impatient for me to catch on.

"Ordered Chinese food?"

"Just come with me," Zanny said, grabbing my wrist.

I pointed to the socks on my feet. "Do you mind?"

"Zanny?" Robin called, from the kitchen. "Is that you?"

I pulled on my sneakers, but Robin was already on us.

"Where are you guys going?" she asked, standing in the doorway.

"Out," I said.

"We need to do some research," Zanny told her.

"On a Saturday night?" Robin asked.

"If Dad gets home, tell him I'll be back by eleven," I said.

In the car, Zanny explained that Phil Girardi made deliveries for The Hidden Panda, and he'd just dropped off some mushu pork and kung po chicken at Ms. Farling's apartment on Pine Street.

"Phil called to tell you this?" I asked. "Don't people think it's a little weird, how interested you are in Ms. Farling?"

"I told them I thought she was a Druid."

"Zanny."

"You think I should tell them she's screwing a student?"

"She's not screwing a student! You'd better stop getting your hopes up."

"PVW 658," Zanny said.

"What?"

"Bertram's license plate."

"Oh, my God."

"It's a silver Passat. Keep your eyes open." We were driving slowly down Pine, which was lined with parked cars along both sides of the street. Zanny pointed over to the Underwood Apartment Building. "She's 6C."

"This is ridiculous."

Zanny's cell phone started playing Beethoven. Da-da-da-dum.

"Hello? Druid hotline," I said, shaking my head.

"Hello?" Zanny said into her phone, pulling over and stopping beside a blue Chevy. I took a deep breath, looking out the windshield and seeing a green Volvo parked in the dark across the street between two streetlights. It looked a lot like Dad's car, but he'd gone out with some guys from work, and Mr. McGuire always drove because he didn't drink.

"Robin?" Zanny said, into the phone.

"What?" I asked. "Robin? As in Robin my sister? What does she want?"

Zanny covered up the phone and told me to shut up.

"What is she doing with your number, anyway?"

"What is it?" Zanny said, into the phone. I watched her, and suddenly her eyes changed.

"What."

"Why do you want to know?" Zanny asked.

"What do you mean? What does she want to know?"

Zanny fell back against the seat. "Oh, my God."

"What. What is going on? Zanny?"

"Oh—my—God." She sounded horrified.

"Will you—?" For some reason I looked back at the green Volvo. Now it was my turn to fall back against the seat.

Jake.

It wasn't Bertram. It was Jake.

I kept looking at the green Volvo. That was Dad's car. It had to be. Jake even had an extra key for it that no one knew about.

"We're leaving right this second," Zanny said, into the phone, and shut it off and put the car back in drive without saying a word.

"What is going on?" I asked.

Zanny said nothing, just accelerated down the street. I looked at the green car as we went by, but it was too dark to see anything.

"Can you slow down?"

"No," Zanny said, white-knuckling the wheel.

"Can you tell me what the hell's going on?"

"Talk to your sister," Zanny said, sounding like someone had died.

I looked out at the street racing into our headlights and felt my stomach sinking. For Zanny, this was like someone had died. Jake. Her beloved Jake. Zanny had thought she was in the inner circle of his life, and now she'd found out he had a secret life she knew nothing about. It didn't matter if Jake and Ms. Farling were screwing or just sharing poetry. There was an inside to Jake's life where Zanny hadn't been invited.

She pulled into our driveway and I got out without a word. Tore off my jacket as I came through the front door and marched through the empty kitchen and opened the door to the garage. No car.

"Jim?" Robin called, from the family room.

I walked back through the kitchen and bounded up the stairs. I could hear Jake's music, could feel it vibrating through his door, but that didn't fool me. I charged toward his door and threw it open.

And saw Jake lying there on his bed, holding his guitar.

Eleven

How could I have been so wrong? I was positive, absolutely positive it was Jake. It just fit, like little plastic pieces of a toy truck snapping together. The phone call from Robin. The freak-out from Zanny. It had to be Jake. It didn't make sense, the world just didn't make sense if it wasn't Jake, if Jake was sitting there in his room.

Looking back on it now, of course, it all makes sense, only in a totally different way. I can look back and think, God, what an idiot. It's so easy to see. How could I not have seen it? What had I been thinking? But it feels like I could do that for almost anything. There's so much that made sense, so much that seemed like a good idea at the time.

Falling in love.

Becoming rich and famous.

Touring the country with Zanny.

Getting kissed by different women.

Acting shy about women's underwear.

Keeping my mouth shut when I found out the real reason women had started kissing me and had started sending me their underwear.

It all made sense at the time, all seemed like the right thing to do. Even this, even now, even sitting here locked in a hotel room in San Diego—it seems right. Even though Mr. Nelson is out there convincing the world I'm wacko, it seems like it makes sense to sit here and finish the story. But there's this voice in the back of my head that keeps wondering—what am I going to regret next? What do I not know? What do I not understand?

What's the next thing that's going to make me feel like an idiot?

"**S**urprise," Jake smiled, just sitting there on his bed holding his beat-up guitar.

All I could do was stand there. I'd been so positive it was Dad's car, so positive it was Jake, back at Ms. Farling's, eating Chinese food. So positive Jake was the reason Zanny was so upset.

I turned and headed for the stairs.

"Nice talking to you," Jake called after me.

Robin was sitting cross-legged on the floor in the family room, meditating. She had the whole thing going—eyes closed, hands held out at her sides, fingers curled like she was saying OK.

"Why did you call Zanny?" I asked.

Robin didn't flinch, didn't move.

"Why do you even have her number?"

"I don't," Robin said, keeping her eyes closed, her voice soft and sleepy, like she was trying to maintain some kind of vegetative state. "I got the number from her mom and dad."

"My phone was on, you know."

Robin lifted her chin up, as if that made her healthier. "You weren't the one I wanted to talk to," she said, her eyes still closed.

"Why not?" I asked. I felt like a little kid again, asking a question about sex or murder—some question the adults would try to ignore. "Why can't you tell me?"

"It's not my job."

"Then whose job is it?"

Robin inhaled through her nose.

"Look. You told freaking Zanny."

"I had no choice," Robin said. "I had to get you out of there."

I stood there watching Robin breathe. "Is Ms. Farling a lesbian?"

Robin opened her eyes, put her hands on her hips. "James."

"It's got to be something like that," I said. "Lesbian or pregnant or... some sort of thing that you'll talk to Zanny about but you won't talk to me about."

Robin just stared at me. "This isn't about you, Jimmy," she said, and closed her eyes and held her hands back at her sides. "The whole world is not about you."

I stood there and gave her the finger. Of course it wasn't about me. It was about Ms. Farling. It was about Ms. Farling, and it was about

Zanny knowing what the hell was going on with Ms. Farling when I didn't.

"Is she a lesbian?"

I asked the next day when we were in the cafeteria. Zanny was scribbling madly in her notebook, which was really annoying because I knew she was writing about whatever the hell was going on with Ms. Farling. Had Zanny found her perfect story? The one that was going to make her famous? Bertram and Ms. Farling weren't having sex, but had Robin told her something else that was going to be Zanny's perfect story?

"A prostitute?" I asked. "Is she a prostitute?"

"Will you go away?"

"I don't care if she's a prostitute," I said. "Why does Robin think I would care if Ms. Farling was a prostitute?"

Zanny didn't lift her head up to look across the table at me. "She's not a prostitute. And she's not a lesbian."

"A communist?" I looked at Gene. "Are there still communists?"

"I have no idea," Gene said, his body tense from listening. He'd switched over to Zanny's side of the table so that he didn't have to face table six, but now he spent lunch listening intently to the cackling behind him.

"Robin knows lesbians. She probably knows communists. Who else would Robin know? Vegetarians?"

Zanny had gone back to her scribbling. I couldn't believe she was doing this to me.

"Why won't you tell me?" I asked, watching her. "I thought we were friends."

"What?" Zanny asked, not looking up, still writing. "Did you say something?"

"Can't you just stop and tell me?"

"Can you two just shut up and eat lunch?" Gene asked, sitting back, tilting his head slightly, listening to snickers from table six.

"Zanny—"

"Look. Relax," she said, leaning across the table, almost whispering. "You'll find out soon enough."

What the hell did that mean? How was I going to find out soon enough? Was Zanny going to make that my Christmas present? Telling me what was going on with Ms. Farling?

I didn't have time to obsess about it. Christmas was scaring me.

First, the day before break, Mr. Grout was giving us his famous Stomp-on-Your-Brain midterm.

Second, we absolutely, positively needed to have all our lines down cold before break or supposedly Mr. Fricker would foam at the mouth.

Third, what was I going to get Zanny, and what the hell was Kurtz going to get her?

And fourth, Mom.

Ever since she left, Robin and Jake had been going over to Stormy Tidewater's house to see Mom three or four times a week, and on a daily basis Dad was pressuring me to go with them. The week before break he started in about Christmas Eve, about how Mom was my mother, and there was no choice, I had to see her for Christmas. Dad even started to cry, which I thought sucked, but it worked.

"I'll go, I'll go, I'll go!" I told him, stomping out of the room.

Mr. Grout's test was the longest forty-five minutes of my life, but I survived, and rehearsal after school was nerve-wracking, but apparently everyone did an adequate job because Mr. Fricker didn't have a nervous breakdown.

Christmas Eve day I took out some of my college money and got Zanny a *Life is Wonderful* baseball cap from me and this idiotically expensive cashmere sweater from Kurtz. Before dinner I went over to Zanny's house for eggnog with her and her parents, and I gave her the baseball cap and she gave me a book of poetry. Afterwards, I went out to my car, grabbed the box with the sweater in it, and stuck it in the front seat of Zanny's Saab, which was parked in the driveway.

> From: kurtz4now@netmail.com
> To: suzannah007@netmail.com
> Date: 24 December 5:46 pm
> Subject: Ho Ho Ho

> Check your car.
>   Love, Santa

I was jittery but felt pretty good, driving with Robin and Jake over to see Mom. It'd put me in the Christmas spirit, buying Zanny the sweater, and I'd bought Mom a bottle of Eve L'Enfant perfume. Jake and I used to love spraying her with the stuff before she and Dad went out, and smelling it at the counter at the mall had reminded me of Mom all dressed up and babysitters and pigs-in-a-blanket, which Mom always let us have because she figured we deserved a treat.

Mom cried when she saw me, and she hugged me an extra long time, but I couldn't tell her to stop because I had this huge lump in my throat. Stormy Tidewater stood there, waiting, and when Mom finally let go of me she rushed at us with big hello's like she was greeting the President and his entourage, her arms waving around, her huge red dress flowing around her.

When I handed Mom her present, it occurred to me that she didn't smell like Eve L'Enfant.

Did she not wear it anymore?

Did the tall man with the palm tree not like Eve L'Enfant?

Mrs. Tidewater led us to the dining room, which was lit by candles everywhere. The table was covered with casseroles and pies and evergreen branches tied up with red ribbons. But there was no tall man with a palm tree, thank God. I almost asked Mom where she put the palm tree, but she was dabbing at her eyes with a paper napkin decorated with a picture of holly.

Mom had baked a lobster quiche, which had somehow become the traditional Christmas Eve dinner at our house, back when we were still a family. She'd cooked the quiche and the yams with the little melted marshmallows and she'd even made an enormous gingerbread house and had all the little cups of different colored icings set up so we could decorate it after dinner, which was another of our Christmas Eve traditions.

I got choked up, looking at the gingerbread, my breathing sounding like Darth Vader's.

We said a weird grace, holding hands around the table, Mrs. Tidewater talking about the Feminine Force of Life. Mom's hand was cold and goose bumps shivered down my back like I was touching a dead body.

As soon as everyone started eating, Mom went into her milk-and-cookies mode, asking us questions like she used to ask questions when we got home from school. Back then, when we got off the bus, Mom never asked dumb how-was-your-day or what-did-you-do questions—they were easy to avoid answering—Mom always wanted to know what was fun, or what was the most interesting thing that happened at lunch, or what was the word problem on the math test.

Sitting there eating the lobster quiche, though, Mom didn't sound like Mom at all. Not when she was talking to me, anyway. I kept getting the feeling I was a foreign exchange student, Mom acting all polite and helping me along as I talked, providing me with words, like she thought English was my second language.

She asked me a lot of questions about *A Midsummer Night's Dream*, but it was like she wanted me to give her the Monarch Notes. I kept having to tell her that I didn't know, I didn't know, I didn't know.

Then she started to cry again. I didn't even notice, at first, but Mrs. Tidewater came over and gave Mom a big hug and that's when I saw the tears.

Robin and Jake were already up and Mrs. Tidewater got out of the way so all three of us could give Mom a hug as she sat there. That made the crying worse, and Mom knocked over her wine, the dark red spill soaking into the white tablecloth.

"I'm sorry, I'm sorry, I'm so sorry," Mom said, laughing and wiping tears, the three of us crowding around her, Mrs. Tidewater on the other side of the table now, smiling at us like she wished she had a camera.

Then the stupid cell phone rang and, as if in slow motion, Mrs. Tidewater reached over to the side table to answer it.

"Hello?" she said, and there was a pause, and then her body twisted away. "Oh, hi, Don," her voice unnatural, like she was reading from a script. I held my breath. Everybody seemed to be holding their breath.

"Oh, well, uh—" Mrs. Tidewater walked into the kitchen, her voice lower. "She can't come to the phone right now, Don, but I can have her. . ." Mrs. Tidewater's voice trailed off as she walked through the kitchen into the hallway.

Don. So. The tall man with the palm tree had a name.

His name was Don.

I stood up straight and crossed my arms. Don the palm tree guy.

"I need to get something outside," I said, and walked through the kitchen and down the hall, grabbing my jacket on the way out.

I felt like I'd lost Mom. The way she was treating me like a guest, the way she'd forgotten how to talk, the way she'd run off with Don the palm tree guy. I didn't even recognize her anymore, wouldn't have been able to pick her out of a crowd.

I buried my hands deep in my pockets and walked fast through the biting cold. I had no idea what I was going to say to Dad. He was going to want to know what happened, what was wrong. What the hell could I say without telling him about Don the palm tree guy?

But Dad never asked.

When I came through the front door Dad came rushing out of the family room.

"You're back so soon," he said, his face flushed. "What time is it? Does anybody have a watch on? I thought you guys would be there for hours!"

What the hell? I wanted to ask how many beers he'd had, and I wandered toward the family room, expecting to see it littered with beer bottles. Instead I saw a fire in the fireplace and a bottle of wine sitting on the floor in front of it. Next to it were two wine glasses.

"Jimmy? Jim!" Dad had gone to the front door, looking for Robin and Jake, and now he was charging back toward the family room. "Can you help me—? There's some presents—"

He may have said more but I didn't hear it. I was walking into the family room, walking toward the heat of the fire, when I saw her, standing in the corner of the room, reading titles from the bookcase.

Ms. Farling.

Twelve

I'm screwed.

Fifteen minutes ago I sat in my hotel room watching Mr. Nelson and Dr. Hackinfire on the Entertainment News Network explaining why I'm so flipped out.

According to them, sudden fame is practically impossible to deal with. For weeks now, they claim, I've been demonstrating erratic behavior, showing signs of sudden attention disorder. Dr. Hackinfire said he couldn't discuss specifics because I was a patient, but Mr. Nelson was happy to talk about the strange disappearance of my laptop in Minneapolis, shaking his head as he talked about my claim that someone had snuck into my room while I was slept and stole it.

"They DID!"

"Hotel security maintained it was impossible, given the lock configuration on the door, but Jimmy continues to insist his laptop was stolen." Mr. Nelson sighed and shook his head. "I spoke with him the next morning, and he sounded remarkably distant, disconnected from the whole incident."

"Because I knew you were the one who got the thing stolen in the first place!" I shouted, jabbing my finger at the television.

Mr. Nelson rolled his eyes slowly, sadly. "Just the day before, of course, Jimmy had disappeared for twelve hours in Dallas."

Sitting here, thinking about it, I slap my forehead. I'm screwed. America's going to believe them, I know it. Who're you going to believe? A world-famous Hollywood agent and a world-renowned psychologist? Or some kid who has locked himself in a San Diego hotel room so he could write a book about how his girlfriend is secretly in love with his twin brother and his world-famous Hollywood agent hired someone to steal his laptop. If Zanny believes them, if they've convinced Zanny that I'm crazy, then of course America's going to think I'm crazy.

OK, look. Yes, I did disappear in Dallas. I was desperate to get away after Zanny finished telling me what an idiot I was for not realizing that all the kissing and all the underwear had simply been publicity stunts orchestrated by our agent. I took off running for the stairs, couldn't deal with seeing her, being around her. And in 106 degree heat, I wandered around downtown Dallas. Stopped for some Mexican food and ice-cold Coke and wondered about all the kisses Zanny had seen, all the underwear I'd shown her. It seemed amazing that Zanny wouldn't say something, wouldn't tell me. It made me wonder who Zanny was. Was Zanny really Zanny? I wanted to believe she was, I wanted to be convinced that deep down inside, Zanny was still Zanny.

That's love for you. Maybe.

It was freaky, on Christmas Eve, seeing Ms. Farling standing there in the corner of my family room, her shirt tail hanging out. Freaky, shaking her hand and wishing her a Merry Christmas.

As soon as Ms. Farling left, Dad was in a hurry to explain everything. Everything. How back in November Mom had forgotten her glasses and had come back inside and had overheard a phone conversation Dad was having with Ms. Farling. How Dad had met Ms. Farling last spring when he'd gone to the high school to deal with something Jake had said to his gym teacher. How they'd started e-mailing each other and how it was all very innocent, and how it probably would have stayed innocent if they hadn't bumped into each other in the bookstore over in Hamden.

Dad somehow knew all about Don, too. Don McMillan, a college friend of Stormy Tidewater's who had made a bazillion dollars in New York but now wanted to find his inner self. He'd been there at Mrs. Tidewater's house the night Mom had shown up in tears after overhearing Dad's phone call to Ms. Farling.

"OK, OK, OK," I said, holding my hands up, wanting to get away from Dad as soon as I could. I got up to my room and closed the door and wrapped my arms around the top of my head. I didn't get it, didn't get it at all. He loved Mom. Didn't he love Mom? What about that night at the restaurant, when he'd had the martinis and wouldn't shut up about staying awake all night, thinking about Mom? He'd loved her—real love, stupid love.

What happened?

The next morning didn't feel much like Christmas. I just stayed in bed for a long time, and then reached over to the nightstand and grabbed the book of poetry Zanny had given me. What was she thinking, poetry? I hated poetry.

Life in the Light of Day. By some Hungarian guy whose last name started with M.

I opened it up and read the inscription.

> *Jim,*
> *To the poet in hiding. Merry Christmas.*
> *I love you,*
> Z

I sat up. Oh, my God. I read it again, just to make sure I got it right. There it was, in blue ink. "I love you." The three words. Oh, my God. I looked around my room, looked back at the book. The three words. I closed the book and started to count to ten. I made it to eight and opened the book up. "I love you."

I swallowed. "Calm down," I said out loud. "Just calm down."

Friends said that kind of stuff to each other. Especially girls. They said that kind of stuff all the time. This wasn't the three words. This was just whatever it was.

"Oh, my God," I told myself, closing the book again as if I was afraid of someone else reading it.

Ten days later, back in the cafeteria, I asked Zanny, "What's she see in my Dad anyway?" I was watching Zanny as much as I could get away with.

"Are you kidding? He's cute," she said, scooping the green fruit out of her kiwi. Who the hell ate kiwi in a high school cafeteria?

"Cute?" This was not something I wanted to hear about my Dad. "I'm not talking about cute. I'm talking about what do they have to say to each other? What do they have in common? Dad's a freaking accountant."

"Are you saying your father isn't good enough for Ms. Farling?"

"What? No," I said, although, really, that was pretty much exactly what I was saying.

"Neil's going to the play," Gene said, folding up his sandwich wrapper. "Did I tell you he's going to the play? Neil? He's driving down all the way from Connecticut for the Saturday night show."

We'd started sitting on the other side of the cafeteria because as soon as Gene found out that Mary was dating a guy from Connecticut named Neil who she'd met on the Internet, he decided he wanted to pretend Mary did not exist.

"He's coming to the cast party," Gene said, still folding his wrapper, which had now taken on the shape of a small cube.

Zanny elbowed him. "What about that girl Bertram wants you to meet?"

"What girl?" I looked at the two of them. How did Zanny find out this stuff?

"Bertram said there's a girl from Passaic he wants Gene to meet."

"He said she was funky," Gene said.

I leaned across the table. "Funky?"

Zanny kicked at me but missed.

"What," I said. "Bertram wears a cape. Is she funkier than a kid who wears a cape?"

"I can't believe he's coming to the cast party," Gene said, not listening.

It may have been easy in the cafeteria for Gene to pretend Mary did not exist, but in the play they were still Theseus and Hippolyta, they were still this couple getting married. In the play Gene still had to hold a big wooden scepter and parade around arm-in-arm with Mary in a wedding march.

"This is a HAPPY thing!" Mr. Fricker screamed at him a week before the show, jumping up on stage and charging toward Gene like he was going to tackle him. "THIS IS NOT A FUNERAL MARCH! Marriage is a good thing to you! You LOVE this woman!" Mr. Fricker jabbed a finger at Mary. "You can't wait for your wedding night! Do you understand that? DO YOU UNDERSTAND YOU CAN'T WAIT TO GET YOUR HANDS ON THIS WOMAN? DO YOU UNDER-STAND HOW HAPPY YOU ARE?"

Gene's lips were tightly closed as he stood there perfectly still. Then suddenly he was swinging the scepter, smashing it down on the stage, the ball at the top popping loudly as it splintered.

No one moved.

Beverly Tungsten, the stage manager, quietly came over and pulled Mr. Fricker aside. Beverly knew everything about everybody, so she must have explained to Mr. Fricker what was going on with Gene and Mary. Mr. Fricker decided they could skip the scepter, and he kept his mouth shut around Gene.

He screamed enough at everyone else, though, to make up for it. That last week before opening night, he wouldn't shut up.

"FIND A WAY TO FIND YOURSELF," he said, his voice getting hoarse as he gave us another one of his lectures on how to get into the roles we were playing. "Love. Jealousy. Remorse. Find out what you can do, how you can spend your spare time tapping into what your character is feeling."

For me, this was no problem: I read poetry. The poems Zanny gave me. *Life in the Light of Day.* They were great poems, incredible poems. I read the poems, and I read the inscription, and then I lay on my bed, thinking. Did she really think I was a poet? Did she really think there was something secret inside me?

What was the "I love you" all about?

Kurtz stopped worrying about what he was saying. He went wild, e-mailing Zanny, talking about a full heart, talking about love, talking about making love. He wrote words I never would have written, never would have said, even if Zanny and I were going out, even if we were lovers.

Playing a character who is madly in love was easy. Zanny and I were never in a scene together, but she was around, I knew she was there, I could feel her presence. I didn't have to tap into how my character was feeling. I was feeling it.

At dress rehearsal, Mr. Fricker went around the circle, telling each of us what we did wrong, but he skipped right over me. "You suck," Bertram whispered.

Opening night was even better. A bunch of freshman girls came backstage after the show, asking me to sign their programs. Mom was there and cried, watching them, and then cried more when she hugged me. Things had been good with Mom since Christmas Day, when I'd gone over and apologized to her for being so mad at her when it turned out Dad was the one being the complete jerk.

More girls crowded around me after the show Saturday night, asking for my autograph. Dad was there, smiling a that's-my-boy smile that really pissed me off. He was having an affair—he didn't have the right to be happy. It bugged the hell out of me, seeing either Dad or Ms. Farling smile or laugh. You have an affair that destroys a family, and you should be miserable the rest of your life, that's all there is to it.

I told Dad I had to go to the cast party and walked away without saying good-bye.

Cast parties were famous at Bedford, and people had been talking about this one for weeks. Bertram claimed the *Oliver* cast party the year before had changed his life. To me, a life-changing party sounded like a good thing.

What did I know?

Zanny was supposed to give me and Gene a ride, but Gene didn't want to wait and got a ride with Beverly Tungsten. So Zanny and I went by ourselves, Zanny smelling like a new shampoo or perfume, the two of us squinting at the rain that looked like snow in the headlights. I was so happy it was disgusting; I couldn't decide which was better, looking over at Zanny in the darkness or looking through the windshield, just knowing she was there.

The party was at Tim Wood's house, around back, where there was a door to the unfinished basement. Everything was dark and the music was so loud it seemed to grab hold of you as soon as you stepped inside. People were dancing near the stairs, and I could see Gene over there, standing against the wall, stiff, like his back hurt. I turned to find Zanny, but she'd disappeared. I fought off a sinking feeling in my heart and headed over to Gene.

Who had a beer. Gene Cooper was drinking a beer.

I nudged him and pointed with my thumb. "What if Tufts finds out?" I hollered.

Gene just nodded, not looking at me. I followed his eyes out to the dance floor and saw Mary, hair flying as she danced with Neil. I didn't remember her ever dancing like that with Gene, and it made me want to go out there and do something. Cut off her hair, stomp on Neil's toes, something.

Zanny appeared with three beers and handed them out. I couldn't believe it—first Gene, and now Zanny, who never drank at parties because she'd read some article in *The New York Times* about high school girls doing incredibly dumb things when they got drunk at parties. So why all of a sudden was it OK? I looked at her, and I struggled for air. She had never looked so beautiful, and I drank my beer fast, thinking about quoting one of the poems from the book she gave me.

> *". . . in the lost garden petals open for the first time. . ."*

I laughed out loud, safely drowned out by the music. God, no wonder people drank beer. I wanted another one, but I didn't want to give up this moment, right here, standing beside Zanny. I didn't want to leave and risk her not being there when I got back, but I was buzzed enough to know that if she was going to leave, she was going to leave, and if she was going to stay. . . .

"I'll be right back!" I hollered to her, feeling like a Zen master as I walked away. OK, where the hell was the beer? I'd be OK with Zanny not being there when I got back. I would. Especially if I could just keep drinking beer until I passed out. But there was no reason she wouldn't be there, if I could just find the freaking beer.

There. In the corner.

I squeezed by a few people and grabbed four cans—one for each of us and a spare because I didn't want to go through this again in another ten minutes. I held three cans in my left hand and popped the fourth one open with my right. Between the crowd and the beer and feeling my body move to the rhythm of the screaming music, it felt like that party was the center of the universe. I'd drunk maybe half the beer by the time I could see Gene.

And there was Zanny, standing there beside him.

"Oh, my God," I said. God, life was good. Life was so good. I felt so buzzed I wondered if I'd ingested something more than beer, if there was some sort of mist that could be sprayed without you noticing.

Zanny and Gene were shouting at each other over the music. I handed out the beers and stood there but could not hear a word, so I kept drinking my beer, glad I'd gotten that spare so I didn't have to leave again. I didn't want to go anywhere. I could have stood there all night looking at Zanny and Gene screaming at each other.

I popped open the last beer just as Zanny leaned toward me like she wanted a kiss.

"Have you seen Bertram?" she shouted.

I shook my head. "Is he bringing Funky Girl?"

She stared at me. "Will you stop?"

Oh, my God, I wanted to kiss her, I so wanted to kiss her. "What. I want to meet Funky Girl."

Zanny just looked at me funny, and I looked back at her. I could do that now. I had no problem looking her square in the eye, and she was looking back at me but I was smiling wildly because I could tell for absolute certain she had no clue.

"So what are you thinking?" I shouted, wanting to make sure she could hear me, but scared that she might give me an honest answer. I wasn't ready for an honest answer. I was close. One more beer and I would have been ready for the truth, but not quite yet. Right now I wanted to keep dreaming, maintain the illusion. One of the poems in the book Zanny had given me talked about illusion, and that was what I was fine with. It was funny, in fact, it was a riot, that we were standing here looking at each other and Zanny had no idea what I was thinking, no idea how much I felt.

She looked away, finally, and elbowed me because there was Bertram standing beside a girl wearing a spiked dog collar and a tight purple velvet bodice thing that showed off her cleavage.

Funky Girl! I almost shouted. This was Funky Girl!

Her nose was pierced and an eyebrow was pierced, but she shook Bertram's hand like a normal human being, like I never would have imagined someone wearing a spiked dog collar would. Maybe I don't know people, I thought. Really. Zanny, even, maybe I didn't even know Zanny, and I turned to ask her about this, but she was gone. Shit. I spun my entire body around, like a batter taking a mighty swing but striking out. Where'd she go? How did that happen? It felt like a magic trick. Did Gene see what happened? I looked at him, but he and Bertram were surrounding Funky Girl and not paying attention to the rest of the world.

A finger appeared in front of my face, a pointing finger, and I thought Zanny was back, but no, it was Janine Johnson, Jake's girlfriend. What the hell was she doing here?

"You—look soooo much like your brother. . ." The finger swayed, but Janine brought it back to point at my nose. She was smashed. She stared at me, thinking for a while before she leaned over close to my ear. "I bet we could have sex and I would never know."

"Yeah," I said, clearing my throat, not sure of the best thing to say and looking at Gene and then Bertram, who were both staring at me.

"You have a solid blue aura," Gene shouted, and pointed his thumb at Funky Girl. "Corrine can see auras. You're solid blue."

I looked at Funky Girl. She was staring at me like Mom used to stare at paintings in museums.

"Quite unusual," Bertram said, with a smile that could have gone a lot of different ways.

Janine grabbed my arm and held on, balancing herself. "Can I talk to you?" she asked, pulling me away.

I looked for Zanny as Janine pulled me around to the other side of the staircase, where there was some shelter from the music and we didn't have to yell so loud. Janine looked up at me and then grabbed my beer and took a swig.

"Are you in love?"

"What?" I asked, squinting, shaking my head like I couldn't hear a thing.

Janine shoved the beer at me. "People in the play think you're in love," she said. "Bertram thinks you're in love. He says that's why you can play that part you're playing."

I took a swig from the beer. "Are you in love?"

She lost her balance and I had to reach over and grab her arm. "Maybe you should get some fresh air," I told her.

"You're sweet," she said, patting my arm.

"Is Jake here?" I asked. "You want me to get him?"

Janine violently shook her head from side to side. "That's not a good idea."

"Let me just find Jake," I said, looking around but not seeing him. Suddenly Janine grabbed my sleeve and twisted it.

"Listen to me," she said, almost desperate. "You haven't seen him with her."

"What?"

She shook her head and leaned forward, resting her head against my chest. "Let's dance."

I needed to find Jake. I looked around, desperate to find Jake, and saw Mary coming down the stairs. I reached through the bars of the handrail and flagged her down. "Have you seen Jake?" I yelled up at her.

She was on the third or fourth step and stopped and blinked twice, staring at me. "Asshole," she said.

"What?" I hollered at her, but then realized I couldn't have heard right. What did Mary have against me?

I didn't know that, ten minutes before, while Mary was in the bathroom, Bertram had pulled aside Neil, Mary's Connecticut boyfriend. He told Neil about the sexual favor Mary had granted Gene back in December. I also didn't know that Neil had just asked Mary about it upstairs, and that Mary had assumed that I was the one who had told Neil.

So I had no idea why Mary had just called me an asshole. I just figured I didn't hear right.

"Jake!" I hollered up at her. "Have you seen Jake?"

Mary pushed her hair back as she bent down toward me, talking through the bars, spitting out the words. "He's making out with Zanny."

The words radiated through me, changing me at the molecular level. By the time I got my balance back, Mary was gone.

Of course, now I understood. I understood everything. Why Zanny was drinking. Why Janine was drinking. Why Zanny disappeared. Why Janine didn't want me to go looking for Jake and was standing here, hiding against my chest. I felt like I understood the entire world, felt like I'd grown up all at once, in the blink of an eye. I could see it all, the whole world.

It never occurred to me, never crossed my mind that Mary might be lying.

"Hey," I said, looking down at the top of Janine's head. "Hey, I need to go."

Janine looked at me, swaying slightly. "Go where?"

"Out," I said, pushing her away and finishing off my beer as I headed for the door and found my jacket in a pile of coats. I couldn't believe how hot it was. The place was a freaking oven, and I burst through the door and sucked in the cold air, a loud rush in my ears as I marched up the driveway, hearing a girl behind me calling my name. I almost ran, just wanted to be out of it, be away from it. It was Janine, rushing to catch up. Janine, who stopped me and talked to me and then kissed me, kissed me hard, and whispered something in my ear, two words, a suggestion that I never believed a girl or a woman would ever say to me in my entire life.

Thirteen

Zanny felt terrible about what happened in Dallas on our tour.

I got back to the hotel after midnight, and she was sitting there in the lobby, and actually came over and hugged me and held my hand and led me over to this enormous brown suede couch and sat me down.

"I should have told you," she said. "I should have just told you."

Mr. Nelson paid that woman in New York to kiss me. And he paid the woman in Hoboken. Then he made sure there was plenty of publicity about strange women coming up and kissing me, and after that women started doing it all on their own.

The same thing happened with the underwear. Apparently, Mr. Nelson sent the first two dozen pair and then leaked the story to *People* about how women had started sending me their underwear. After that it caught on.

Zanny told me everything, sitting there, holding both my hands, apologizing, brushing hair off my forehead, apologizing again.

It mattered to her. I mattered. She cared, I thought, really cared. At one point, she kissed me on the cheek, she brushed her lips against mine, looking ready to cry. This was Zanny—Zanny, about to cry. I'd never felt so important. Had never, in my entire life, felt so close to her.

So it seemed kind of amazing that the very next day, in Minneapolis, Zanny would believe hotel security instead of me; would believe I was wacko because I thought someone had snuck into my room and stolen my computer.

And it seems even more amazing that just a week later—about ten minutes ago—someone slid under my door a note in Zanny's handwriting.

Dear Jim,
Please come out. Please get help. Please.
Love,
Z

Outside the party, Janine had me call a cab and then pushed me up a car parked in the driveway. I had no idea kissing could be so. . . erotic. Janine grinding against me, moving my hands where she wanted them, making sounds. The taxi driver had to honk to get our attention.

"My place is a mess," Janine said, as we climbed into the cab.

Her place. Janine had her own place. And the two of us were going there. If I hadn't had any beer, I wouldn't have believed any of this. I would have been sure Janine was pulling my leg. It was the drinking that made it all seem possible.

"You have any beer?" I asked. "At your place?"

Janine snorted a laugh and patted my thigh and climbed up and straddled my lap, facing me. I wasn't delusional, I knew Janine wasn't kissing me because she'd been dying to kiss me, just like I knew that Rita, the woman who cleaned our house, wasn't cleaning houses because when she was little she always hoped she could grow up and clean houses. Sometimes things just happen in ways you never expected. Maybe most of life happens that way, who knows? One thing for sure was that I was touching a naked breast for the first time in my life. No one had ever mentioned how soft it would feel, or how different it was from flesh on any other part of the body.

The cab pulled into the parking lot of Fellini's Paints on Larchmont Avenue. I didn't understand, at first, and thought maybe the cabbie was going to rip us off, but Janine told me she lived in the small apartment over the store. The owner's retarded brother had lived there for many years until he drowned in a bathtub in Atlantic City while his brother was down in the casino playing blackjack.

Janine's door was around back, near the dumpster. The stairs going up to her apartment smelled like they'd gotten three fresh coats of paint that day. Janine wouldn't turn on any lights in the apartment except for a strip of red Christmas lights that were wrapped around a pipe that divided the kitchen from the rest of the place, most of which was taken up with her bed. Janine kicked some clothes into a corner and grabbed a huge armful of clothes off her bed and stuffed them into the closet.

"I basically do two things here," she said, leaping onto her bed with a bounce and looking over her shoulder at me. "Want to make us some drinks?"

There was orange juice in the fridge and a bottle of Bacardi rum under the sink. Janine had one of those under the counter refrigerators, and the freezer door inside was frosted over, so ice was not going to happen. Janine turned on the radio and lit candles and met me on the way back to the bed, sipping from the drink in my left hand and grabbing both drinks because they didn't have enough rum. I sat down on the carpet at the foot of the bed and watched her pour in more Bacardi.

"Whew!" she shouted, sipping from one of the glasses as it sat on the counter. "GODDAM I LOVE BEING ABLE TO BE LOUD!" she screamed, turning up the radio and kneeling down to offer me my drink. "Try it, try it," she said, and I did and could not believe how bad it tasted, and could not believe how warm it felt, and could not believe how fast it was gone. I followed Janine into the kitchen and stood there as she fixed us more drinks.

"I don't—" I cleared my throat. "I'm not sure if I'm supposed to say this or not, but—"

"You're a virgin."

I wiped my mouth. "Yeah, that's pretty much—yeah."

"That's so sweet," Janine said, running her hand along my cheek. "Most guys wouldn't have the balls to admit it."

I took my glass. "Most guys. . .wouldn't have to."

Janine leaned her hip against the counter, sipping her drink as she looked at me. "That's because most guys aren't as nice as you are."

I drank my drink, looking at the floor. "If I was so nice, I wouldn't be here."

Janine reached over and touched my shirt. "You wouldn't be here . . . if a lot of things."

"Did you—? At the party, did you—?"

"Not everything is worth knowing," Janine said.

My eyes didn't move from the floor, but I felt Janine's presence and knew she was one of those people who could see the sadness in things pretty clearly. I felt her hand on my shirt, felt her fingers moving against my chest, and I believed I knew this girl, I understood her in a way I didn't understand her when we climbed the stairs to her apartment, and in a way that I wouldn't understand her when I woke up the next day. But the way I knew her right now, this way I felt about her, no matter how much beer and rum and orange juice I'd had, this way I felt about her, was the right way to feel about her, was what she really was, I knew Janine, I knew who she was and I knew what made her sad.

We drank, sprawled out on the carpet, which smelled like popcorn and dirt. Janine had moved out because of her stepfather, her whole body shivering as she sat there probably thinking about him. Then she was kissing me and clothes were coming off and then Janine told me not to move, to just sit there, and she stood up and removed the rest of her clothes and let me just look at her for a while, and she was beautiful, so beautiful, her skin glowing in the shadowed light.

"I need to go," I realized, and Janine nodded her head.

"In a minute," she said, and knelt beside me and had me lie down and draped her blouse over my face because she didn't want me to watch her.

Oh, my God.

We curled up around each other under a blanket afterwards, and I stared up at the ceiling. Janine seemed to have fallen asleep.

"Not everything was worth knowing."

I didn't completely understand what she was saying, but I knew it was something Janine believed with absolute certainty and would say many times to many people for the rest of her life.

The candles had mostly burned out but the red Christmas lights were bright enough for me to find my clothes. It felt right to be outside in the cold, holding my arms tight to my sides. I walked slowly toward the traffic light up at Tremont, past a cinder block building and a parking lot surrounded by a twelve-foot-high chain link fence. Something made me stop and look over my shoulder, and on the second floor, above the paint store, the light was on. Janine was awake. I stopped walking, could see the wind push gently at the Fellini's Paint Store sign. Had she pretended to be asleep? Just to get me out of there? Why didn't she ask me to leave? Tell me to leave?

The street was so silent I could hear the traffic light behind me click as it changed color. I stared at the light in Janine's window, wishing I was close enough to hit it with a rock. Break it with a rock. Did I want to break it? I turned and tried to just let it go, but the bright window in the dark haunted me. I wanted to talk to her. I wanted to look at her and tell her how sorry I was that I let her do that, that I didn't leave when I knew I should have.

I headed north on Tremont, thinking about calling a cab but feeling like I needed to walk, just walk and walk and remember over and over what I should have done, what should have happened. God, I hoped there wasn't a God, really hoped there wasn't a heaven with Grandma up there watching that.

The blisters started before I got to White Plains Road, and I was limping by the time I finally got to our neighborhood, where there wasn't a single light on until I got to our house. Robin had left the kitchen and front lights on, and there was a car parked out front. I walked past the McDermotts' and stopped dead in the middle of the street. Zanny. It was Zanny's car. In front of our house. At freaking four o'clock in the morning.

I stood there looking at it and felt a coldness filling me up. OK. OK. OK, I kept telling myself. They were in his room but the door was closed. I didn't have to see them. I didn't have to think about them. I didn't have to wonder what the hell was going on in there. I could just go to sleep. That's all. Just get to sleep as long and hard as I could, and then in the morning play loud music in my room until the car was gone. That would work. That would be OK.

My heart felt like a wild machine bolted into my chest as I walked stiffly up the path, ignoring the ache in my legs as I climbed the front steps. My hands shook as I tried to unlock the dead bolt. OK, I told myself one more time, putting my shoulder to the door.

The cold stillness in me had taken over, so I didn't even jump when I saw Zanny standing in the front hall.

I grunted, not even looking at her.

Wham!

It felt harder than the palm of her hand, she hit me so hard. I was too stunned, too furious to move.

"What the f—"

Wham!

On my other cheek, with her other hand. I took a step back through the open door. "What—is—going—on?"

Zanny stared at me with a cold fury of her own. "You love me," she said.

And, like a flash fire, I saw the whole night. I was wrong. Completely wrong. Zanny and Jake hadn't happened. And I'd—I shut my eyes, knowing what I'd done.

Zanny brushed by me and leapt off the steps, headed toward her car. I had nothing to call to her, no way to follow.

Fourteen

It's almost funny, Zanny asking me to leave this hotel room and get help, Zanny sliding that note under my door, Zanny thinking I'm wacked . . .

Funny because she knows the way Mr. Nelson works. She knows he'll twist the truth. She knows he'll do anything to make things look the way he wants them to look.

She knows her first draft of *Love Doesn't Grow on Trees* included an entire chapter about that night of the cast party. Included finding out at the party that I'd left with Janine, included waiting at my house, included how good it felt to slap my face.

She knows Mr. Nelson got the editors to rewrite all that stuff, to gloss over the cast party, cutting out the beer and Janine and slap across my face so the two of us would look like nice, clean-cut American kids.

And she knows me. This is what I don't get. Zanny has known me since we were freaking babies. We walked around naked together. Grew up together. Held hands and talked on a freaking couch in Dallas together. Last week! Just last week Zanny admitted to me all the crap Mr. Nelson was up to.

And now she thinks I'm wacked? A nutcase? When did this happen? When did she come to this conclusion? Minneapolis? Dallas? Before Dallas?

That whole hand-holding, lip-brushing thing on the couch in Dallas. Did she already think I was crazy? Did she already think I needed help?

Maybe I do. Maybe I really need help. Any guy who loves a girl who writes him a note asking him to please get help. Maybe Zanny's right.

Maybe I am wacked.

I grabbed the handrail and pulled myself up the stairs, both cheeks burning, still feeling the sting from Zanny slapping me. I crawled into bed, wanting to sleep for the rest of my life, but my cell phone rang at nine and then ten, and then eleven. Each time I opened my eyes and looked at my clock and stared down at my pants on the floor, surprised the muffled little ringing sound coming from my pocket could wake me up. I stared at my pants and closed my eyes before the ringing even stopped, desperate to just get back to sleep. It was the only way to get away, the only way to forget, although even my subconscious was hounded by guilt. I dreamt about tripping and falling against plants and snapping their stems, and I dreamt about the side of my jaw falling away in my hand, and I dreamt about getting so lost I couldn't even keep track of where I was trying to go.

Still, it was better than being awake. After the eleven o'clock call I had trouble falling back asleep, but I kept my eyes closed, desperate, until I heard the doorbell ring downstairs. I jumped up, squinting out the window, scared it was Zanny but seeing Gene's car. I collapsed back into bed and wrapped my pillow around my head.

Someone pounded on the door. It sounded like a leg of lamb beating against it.

"Go away, Gene."

He opened up the door and stuck his head in. "Robin gave me a letter for you."

I closed my eyes.

"Are you still asleep?"

"Yes."

"You're not going to believe what happened last night."

Gene got laid. I could hear the dumb-luck happiness in his voice. I kept my eyes closed but could hear him sit down at my desk.

"You're really not going to believe it," Gene said. "What an awesome party."

"Maybe we can talk about it tomorrow."

"Where'd you go, anyway?" Gene asked. "You like disappeared and missed everything. Corinne was matching people up by their auras. Only certain auras are compatible. Other auras are just never going to work together. Period."

"Gene—"

"So guess who isn't compatible?" he asked. "Just guess."

"Mary and Neil," I said, my eyes still closed. "Can I go to sleep now?"

"So you know what Bertram did?" Gene asked, starting to laugh. "You're really not going to believe what Bertram did."

"He killed Neil with a blow dart."

"Better than that," Gene said. "He told Neil what Mary did. That—like—sexual thing she did for me the week before we broke up."

This got my eyes open. "What?"

"So Neil asks Mary about it and then goes storming off. He's gone! Period!" Gene tossed the letter from Robin on my desk and slapped his leg. "And then—and then—" Gene was laughing too hard now to talk. "Bertram asks her to dance. Asks Mary, acting all innocent like he knows nothing about what happened with Neil. I guess Mary was convinced you told Neil—"

I sat up. "Wait. Wait. What?"

"Can you believe it? She's crying on Bertram's shoulder about what an asshole you are."

Asshole! She did say asshole!

"By the end of the night Bertram had Mary off in the corner, making out with her."

I stared at Gene. "And you think that's a good thing?"

"Are you kidding me?" Gene asked. "I say ABN. Anybody But Neil."

I rested on my elbow, wishing I could come up with an acronym. Something that would set things right, something that could work that didn't involve sleep.

"Jude also said her aura and my aura have an intense sexual compatibility."

Oh, God, he did get laid. I closed my eyes. "I'm coming down with something," I said, coughing in Gene's direction. "You might want to get out of here."

I couldn't sleep after Gene left, and I sat on the edge of my bed, trying to think of another way to get away. The letter from Robin was sitting on my desk, but I knew reading anything from her was just going to make me feel worse. Maybe that was what I needed, though, maybe that was exactly what I needed, was to feel worse.

I grabbed the note, tore it open. Disappointed. Robin was disappointed in me. When Zanny showed up at the house at two in the morning, Robin knew it was bad, knew I had spent a lot of the night with Janine, but it wasn't until she got Zanny to talk about it that she found out how bad. How could I? With Jake's girlfriend! Did I see the parallel with Mom and Dad, how both Dad and I had betrayed the family and ourselves? Did I understand who I should talk to about this, who I should see? Did I understand how beneficial it could be to both of us, talking to Mom about last night—

Mom?

I reread the last sentence. What was Robin saying? That I should talk to Mom? About what happened after the cast party? What was Robin thinking? Was she on drugs? Mom was the absolute last person I would want to talk to. Who could possibly think anyone would ever want to talk to his mother about something like that? Especially after what happened with her and Dad, how could Robin think I should go over and confess to Mom?

No, what I needed was to be Catholic again. What I needed was to go to confession, to kneel in the black box, and whisper through the grill to some priest I'd never seen before.

"Bless me father for I have sinned."

I'd walk out a free man, slate clean, forgiven. I remembered from catechism class, that was the way it worked. It was like you'd rewound the tape and erased everything.

I wasn't Catholic anymore, though. I was stuck. No slates were getting clean.

I got dressed and snuck out the front door without talking to anyone. I didn't want to see Robin. Or Dad. Or Jake. God, I went down a list and couldn't think of anyone I wouldn't want to avoid for the next several years. I climbed in my car and started driving, feeling mechanical, robotic. It felt all right, better than anything else, and I drove out of town and got on the Garden State Parkway and ended up driving all the way to the ocean, where most everything was deserted. I found a small diner and ordered a bagel with cream cheese and a cup of coffee and felt safe, not knowing anybody. Down on the beach the cold wind whipped around like it was trying to attack me. I walked for a long while, the sky pushing down closer and turning darker gray. Eventually I took my socks and sneakers off and watched my feet change color as I let the frigid waves lap over them.

I used my cell phone to call home and got lucky, the answering machine picking up. I said I was having dinner at Gene's, not caring if they heard the waves crashing in the background. The sky turned charcoal and I was shivering and made it back to my car, where I sat for a long while, my stomach growling, the street lights flickering on.

The diner was closed but I found a gas station convenience store, where I bought a loaf of stale white bread and a jar of peanut butter and a Coke. I climbed back in the car and used a white plastic knife to spread out thick globs of peanut butter, the bread cracking as I folded it.

Dad was waiting in the kitchen when I got home.

"Where were you?" he asked.

"The beach," I said, not looking at him.

He didn't try to say anything, which was good, and in the morning I left for school in the cold dark before anybody else got up. I skipped lunch, hiding in the C-wing back stairway, and then stayed there for English, too. Just sitting, though, was bad. Just sitting left too much wide-open space for thinking, and, after a while, no matter how stupid it sounded, my mind kept coming around to what Robin wrote in her note.

After school I drove around over in Hamden, eating a little more of the white bread and peanut butter, which stuck like paste in my mouth. I parked outside a grocery store and watched the sky go from pink to dark blue to black, the parking lot filling up and then emptying out.

Lights were on at Stormy Tidewater's house, and Mom's car was in the driveway, parked beside Mrs. Tidewater's black Mercedes. The front porch light was on, the steps sanded and salted and dry. I took a deep breath, like I was shooting a game-winning foul shot, and rang the bell. Couldn't hear a thing, except my heart. Then Mrs. Tidewater's triangular face appeared in one of the little windows beside the door, her eyes going wide when she saw me. She flung open the door.

"Jake!"

"Jimmy, actually."

This made her even more enthusiastic. "Jimmy! Of course. How are you? Come in, come in! Isn't that odd," she said, closing the door, and leading me back toward the kitchen. "I had a dream just last night about a stranger coming to the door, not a stranger, really, but some-one who I couldn't see clearly, a man, a man wearing a coat," she said, pointing to my jacket.

Stormy Tidewater saw connections in everything: dreams, dropped spoons, clouds across the sky. Mom thought she was a deeply feeling person; Dad thought it was too many drugs in college.

I held my breath, walking into the kitchen expecting to see my mom, but it was bright and empty. Mrs. Tidewater was talking about some organic peaches she had bought Saturday that turned out to be exactly the color she was looking for in her bedroom, and she quick took the peaches to the paint store and they were able to match them perfectly.

I kept nodding my head. "Is my mom around?"

"Isn't that funny? What is wrong with me?" Mrs. Tidewater threw her hands up, marveling at herself. "Here I am going on and on about peaches, when of course you're here to see your mom. Who isn't even here!"

She had three theories about where Mom was, but then admitted she really had no idea. She thought Mom would be home any minute, however, and I was welcome to stay and wait, if I wanted, would I like some papaya juice, had I ever had papaya and seltzer? I shook my head and said no thanks, but she already had the papaya juice out of the refrigerator and was talking about riboflavin, the vitamin, as she opened cabinets and finally found seltzer.

Mrs. Tidewater's call phone went off, playing the theme from *Close Encounters*. She danced over to answer it.

"Sally, hi!" she hollered. "I'm out the door," she said, starting to unbutton her blouse as she headed back down the hall and up the front stairs. I poured myself some papaya juice, which was thick and sickly yellow-orange. The seltzer made it look better, but I still hadn't tried it by the time Mrs. Tidewater came back downstairs, talking into the phone about some guy who wore a camouflage jacket and com-mando boots.

"Jesus, like some war hero," she said, waving good-bye to me. "Help yourself to anything, Jimmy. Your mom will be so happy to see you. Ciao."

I wasn't planning on staying in the house by myself, but I figured rather than trying to explain that, I'd just wait and then leave right after Mrs. Tidewater. I put the bottles of seltzer and papaya juice back in the refrigerator and decided to throw some ice in my glass before trying the drink.

That's how I found the vodka.

A nearly full bottle of Stoli. I tilted the bottle and looked at the clear liquid slide along the inside of the glass. I pictured the conversation I was going to have to have with Mom, if she got there before I left, and I decided to use the vodka instead of the ice to cool off my drink. Vodka doesn't smell, is what I'd heard, but as soon as I poured it into the papaya and seltzer I could smell it big time, and I put the bottle back and drank fast, opening cupboards, looking for gum or hard candy or something to get the smell off my breath. The papaya was delicious, the bubbly seltzer making it taste like something they'd serve in a fancy restaurant in Florida. Or the Bahamas. Mom and Dad went to the Bahamas all by themselves once. That seemed hard to believe now.

I looked out the front window of the dining room and didn't see any headlights and ran back to the kitchen for some more papaya. I left more room for the vodka this time, and refilled the bottle with water like I'd seen in the movies. As soon as I got it back in the freezer I started drinking the papaya mixture again because I realized I should have made half a drink. Having a whole drink in my hand was just too dangerous, I wouldn't be able to down it in one go. Once the drink was nearly finished I felt safe, and I stopped checking for headlights.

What was Mom's car doing in the driveway, anyway? Whose headlights would be bringing her home? The tall man with the palm tree? Donald? Were Mom and Donald out on a date? Did they go to listen to some lecture at the university? Did they shop together at the health food store?

I finished the drink and decided to make one more half glass, and it was kind of funny because I lost my balance as I poured the seltzer, and then I refilled the vodka bottle. I put in too much water so I ended up having to pour a little more vodka into my drink so that with the papaya and the seltzer, it was almost a whole other drink again. The vodka bottle was wet, now, and slipped out of my hands and crashed to the hardwood floor but did not break, and I thanked God with a sincerity that would have made Grandma proud.

Carefully I stuck the bottle back in the freezer and turned on the fancy radio Mrs. Tidewater had on the countertop. What kind of music did she listen to? I hit the preset buttons—public radio and alternative music mostly. I wondered about her. Did she have sex? I couldn't picture people looking like her having sex, but I imagined it happened once in a while. What did she think her life was going to be like? When she was in high school, did she think she would divorce a rich guy and live by herself in a big house? Or did she think about love? Did she grow up and think she would be in love?

Love. What was it Mr. Fricker said? "Love is lost on us." Isn't that what he said? Love is lost on us. Is that what happened, eventually? Love got lost on us?

Had Mom ever loved Dad? I never heard her talk about it, and I was glad for the papaya drink because I was ready to ask Mom, ready to just come out with it. Did she ever love Dad? Because that could be a problem. If he loved her and somehow won her over, but she never loved him back. That would be awful, awful, awful, if I never saw Zanny again ever it'd be better than Zanny deciding OK, she liked me OK, maybe OK she'd go out with me, and eventually maybe OK she'd marry me.

Is that what happened to Mom? I didn't know how things happened, if Mom and Dad wore each other down, or if Ms. Farling got in the way, or if they wore each other down and Ms. Farling just happened to be there. I really had no idea how any of it worked. In high school did Mom think she was going to live happily ever after? Did she think that it would happen now, with Mr. Donald Palm Tree? Were they going to live happily ever after? Does love stay lost on us? How old was Mr. Fricker? When you got old, was love still lost on us? Oh, thank God I never wrote poems, thank God everything was e-mail, everything was cyberspace, deleted and gone, like words drawn in the sand, without weight or permanence. I loved the Internet, the complete nonpermanence of it. I would have hated to face those words now, in this different state, the words telling a truth that even after all this papaya juice and vodka, I wouldn't want to admit.

The doorbell rang.

The doorbell. Oh, shit. I finished the drink and ran to the sink and quickly rinsed the glass and shook the water out and suddenly the glass shattered. What? I stood there, studying the shards of glass for a clue, and then saw the streak of red on the faucet. Ohhhhhhhh. The glass smashed against the spigot, and the red streak—I swiped at it with my index finger. It was blood. I looked at my chest, my torso first, then saw my right hand, holding what was left of the glass, bright red blood dripping down onto the white porcelain sink. Would it stain? I stuck my left hand under my right to catch the blood drops, but then looked around and couldn't find a trash can.

"Hello?" came from the front door. "Anyone home?"

I looked at my hand, which actually seemed to bleed faster, hearing her voice. "Zanny?"

"What's going on?" she called, still in the front hall. "Robin's been trying to call you."

"I'm not really worrying about Robin right now!" I hollered back, walking full circle around the kitchen looking for the freaking trash can. I was trying to use my foot to open the cabinet under the sink when Zanny appeared in the doorway.

"What is going on with you?" she asked, then saw my hand. "Jesus Christ. What did you do?"

"Could you find the trash?"

Zanny walked toward me, her mouth gaping as she watched the dripping blood. "Oh, my God, you need a doctor."

"I don't need a doctor, I need a trash can!"

"What is that smell?"

"Papaya. It's papaya, OK? Can we focus on a trash can?"

"Have you been drinking?"

"Will you—?" I gave up on Zanny and just dropped the broken glass on the counter. A chunk of glass fell out of my palm and clinked, and now I had a good look at the blood-soaked gash right on my life line. I lost my balance.

"Jesus, Jim, you're smashed. What are you doing? What is wrong with you?"

A small pool of blood was in the palm of my left hand, and I tried to pour it down the drain, but it was thick and didn't pour well.

"Hold still, don't move." Zanny took over, turning on the water and grabbing the wrist of my right hand.

"What are you doing? Wait, no, no. No!"

"Shut up," Zanny said, pulling my hand under the running water. I gritted my teeth, bracing for the pain, but the water felt warm and gentle. "Now watch out," Zanny told me, "there are little shards all over your hand. What the hell were you trying to do?"

"I was trying to clean up because you rang the freaking doorbell," I said, and lost my balance again, trying to look at Zanny without it being obvious.

"You can't even hold yourself up!" Zanny complained, yanking on my wrist again. "What's happened to you?" This last question was not about the cut or even the alcohol, it was about me, she still didn't seem to get what was wrong with me. I watched Zanny studying my hand, squinting to find any remaining slivers. The side of her face this close, the pale skin against her black hair, was beautiful. I wanted good things for her, no matter what, I loved her and I would always love her and I wanted just good things. "Jake loves you," I said.

She kept looking at my hand but slowly nodded. "I know."

This was not what I was expecting. "He told you?"

"None of your business."

"Did he say he loved you?"

"What do you care?"

"What. I'm just curious," I said, trying to keep my voice down, trying not to scream. I didn't understand why I was so angry, but I could feel it, like the hum of a tuning fork buried deep inside me. "I can't picture Jake going around saying I love you. He just doesn't seem the type. I love you. I love you."

"He didn't say it," Zanny told me, letting go of my hand and taking the paper towel roll from the holder.

"He wrote it? In words, he actually wrote it? Those three words? "I love you?" I was ready to scream. "Was it a Hallmark card? With a kitten on the front?"

"What is your problem, Jim?"

"I just want to know. Did it have a kitten on the front?"

"You're bleeding on the floor," Zanny said, throwing the paper towel roll at my head.

She was right about the floor—bright red splatters were all over the place. I bent down and tried to pick up the paper towels, but they unraveled on me and headed toward the table.

"You need to give me your keys."

"What?" I was on my hands and knees, sliding paper towels along the floor, hoping I was getting most of the blood.

"I'm leaving," Zanny said, "but I need your keys before I go."

I kept my head down, looking for drops I missed, and noticed my hand had bled through the toweling and had left a smear as I was wiping.

"Just give me your keys, Jim."

The smear had dried and wouldn't wipe up.

"Jim."

"You know I'm Kurtz," I said, the words amazing me as I heard them.

I wasn't looking up so I couldn't tell what Zanny was doing. "Yes," she said.

I looked down at my bleeding hand and started to laugh. "You know?"

"I saw you put the Christmas present in my car."

Oh, my God. I couldn't move, stayed there on my hands and knees thinking about all the things I wrote. I stared down at the smeared blood on the floor, my skin crawling, humiliated. The words, some of the words—Oh, my God. I suddenly realized there was something important. More important than—Just—If—I held my breath. "It's all deleted, right?"

Zanny didn't say anything.

I swallowed, looked over my shoulder at her. "Zanny—"

"You need to give me your keys."

"You said you deleted everything," I said. "That was the deal."

Zanny nodded.

"You deleted everything?"

She kept nodding.

"It's gone?"

"Jimmy. Give me your keys."

"Wait, wait, wait, wait," I said, using the countertop to pull myself up. "You deleted everything."

"Wrap your hand up, would you please?"

"YOU TOLD ME YOU DELETED EVERYTHING!"

"I DID!" she shouted back. "I deleted everything."

"But what?" I pushed. "What, Zanny?"

"I made a copy."

"What?"

"I printed out a copy."

Holy shit. I felt a wave of cold reaching deep inside. There was only one reason Zanny would do that, one reason she would take the e-mails and print them out. She planned on using them, planned on using the words, planned on taking them for her perfect story, the one that would make her famous.

I made a run for it.

"Jim, where are you going! JIMMY! You can't drive!"

Zanny chased me down the hall and grabbed me as I pulled the door open. Outside Mom was coming up the steps, followed by the tall man with the palm tree, their eyes huge at the sight of us.

"Here, here!" I said, pushing my keys into Zanny's hands and running out and leaping off the steps at an angle, landing in the snow and falling.

"James?" Mom called, but I was up and running hard diagonally across the yard, leaving deep footprints in the snow.

Fifteen

I wish I had a video of what Zanny said on CNN. I'd love to watch it a few times, to study it, to try to see what she's really thinking. I wish I had a video of our conversation on that couch in Dallas. I daydream about some middle-aged balding tourist coming forward with footage he secretly videotaped of our conversation in Dallas. Or even someone who overheard Zanny yelling at me while we were waiting at the elevators. I wish I could talk to someone who overheard Zanny telling me about the kisses and the underwear.

There're a thousand people I wish I could talk to.

The woman from Hoboken Mr. Nelson paid to kiss me.

Or the woman from New York.

Or whoever mailed the underwear for Mr. Nelson. There were different postmarks from all over the country. There has to be a bunch of people who mailed them.

Or whoever stole my computer.

Or even the editors who read Zanny's first draft of *Love Doesn't Grow on Trees.*

They know. They all know. How many people out there could come forward, could prove I'm not completely crazy, could tell the world I'm not making all this up?

Of course only one of them knows me. Only one of them wrote "I love you." Maybe only one of them is my friend. Maybe.

I ran like the wind, as I tore down Thompson and cut through behind the middle school. I'd left my jacket at Mrs. Tidewater's and my shirt was sucking up the frigid air, the skin along my arms itchy with cold, but I knew if I kept running, if I kept this pace I could make it, I could get to Zanny's house first. She didn't know where I was going, and even if she figured it out, I was nearly flying, my stride light and stretched out, like I was in a dream and not quite held down by gravity. Please let me get there first, please let me get there first.

I was desperate to get those words, to destroy them forever. It drove me crazy, that Zanny might publish them, that Zanny might put those words in an article or a book, that other people might read them—Gene or Mary or Ms. Farling or Robin or Mom or Dad or Jake. Jake! I'd have to kill Jake if he read those e-mails. Not to mention the rest of the world! If the entire freaking world got ahold of those words. . .

I ran against the light across Main Street, a couple of cars honking, my lungs burning, pushed by the possibility that these words could be exposed to the world. Zanny would do it, too. She wanted to be famous, she hated me. . . of course she'd do it.

The hill up to Nichols Lane, that was all I had left, but my legs were rubbery and my heart sank with every car that passed me—any one of them could be Zanny.

But they weren't. I got to her house and the driveway was empty. I was ready to have a heart attack, but I didn't stop, I knew the Mannings never locked the front door until everyone was home and I took the front steps in a single bound and threw open the door.

"Suzannah?" Mrs. Manning called, from the den. I could see her turning to look as I darted up the staircase. "Hello? Hello? Zanny?" she said, panic already filling her voice.

I grabbed the banister at the top of the stairs to pull myself up. It wasn't just the running, now, affecting my legs. It was fear. What the hell was I doing? I went into Zanny's room and could hear Mrs. Manning downstairs.

"Frank? Frank, come quick, someone just ran up the stairs. A man, I think. Frank?"

I quickly turned on the light. Computer. Printer. I pulled out papers. Opened folders. They could be anywhere. Anywhere.

"Hello? Hello, who's up there? Who is it?" It was Zanny's dad, calling out from the bottom of the stairs. He sounded angry, but the anger was giving way to fear. I'd never heard him sound scared before. "Margaret, call the police!" he shouted. "You'd better leave! We're calling the police!"

"Shit," I muttered, my head twisting, looking, looking, my eyes locking on the drawer in the nightstand.

I heard a faint siren and felt my knees buckle. I opened the drawer and saw a pink file folder right there on top, and I knew what it was before I opened it. The siren was getting louder and I grabbed the folder and flung it open, the white pages spilling out on the floor. As they landed, I saw enough to know this was what I was looking for, and I dropped to my knees and collected the pages, maybe twenty of them all together, the words large on the pages, huge. Why had she printed them in such in a big font, made them so. . .obvious?

I got to my feet but too late. Outside Zanny's window I saw flashing lights as a cop car pulled up. I looked at the clump of papers in my hand. If I had had a pack of matches, if I could have somehow gotten a fire started, I could have gotten rid of them in the blink of an eye. I thought of the toilet, but what if they clogged it? I couldn't trust flushing them. And if I tore them up, no matter how small, they'd be able to piece everything back together.

Another set of flashing lights pulled up outside. I looked out the window at the figures down there in the front yard, moving in the dark. My eyes opened wide, like a horse's facing a blazing fire. That was when I saw the tree. The oak tree outside Zanny's window that was planted too close to the house. Once, when Zanny and I were ten, we kneeled by her window and dared each other to jump out to a branch.

The tree was six years older now. Six years stronger.

"He's upstairs officer."

I didn't have any other options. I rushed to the window, threw it open and climbed halfway out. Oh, my God. The cold took my breath away, the cold and the distance to the ground and the distance between me and that branch, that branch that was as thick as a thigh, that branch that could hold me, no problem. If I could reach it, reach it and hold on.

"Put yours hands up!" It was the cop, on the stairs. Maybe at the top of the stairs.

I looked down and saw a narrow ledge of an overhang a couple of feet below Zanny's window, and I pushed my foot against it, half hoping it would give and I could climb back in and let the cop handcuff me. But as soon as I pictured that, I pictured him reading the pages.

Showing the pages to Mr. and Mrs. Manning. Maybe even keeping them as evidence.

I stuffed the pages into the front of my pants and, holding on tight to the window frame, I pulled my other leg out and sat down on the window sill.

"Hey you!"

I turned to look over my shoulder and lost my balance when I saw an old cop standing at Zanny's bedroom door, pointing a gun at me. A gun, a freaking gun!

I was falling, slipping off the window sill, and I flung my arm wildly, slapping at the side of the window frame.

"Freeze!" the cop yelled, shaking the gun at me. Not a good idea, to start falling out a window when a cop's got a gun pointed at you.

Oh, Jesus. My breath was quivering with fear, but I knew I was out of time, saw the old cop creeping across the room, his arms locked straight ahead of him, the gun pointed at my head. I looked at the tree.

"It's twenty feet down!" the cop shouted, close now, not needing to shout, but shouting just the same. "You fall wrong, you kill yourself!"

Yeah, well. I heaved myself, threw myself as hard I could toward the tree.

"No!"

I badly miscalculated my jumping ability when completely panicked and slammed into the branch.

"Ugghh."

I felt the pain in my shoulder and ribs and ear only after I'd gotten my legs and arms wrapped around the branch.

"Hold on! Hold on, son!" the cop yelled behind me from Zanny's window.

Well, duh, I wanted to tell him, my cheek pressed against the cold bark as I tried to hook my right leg around far enough to pull myself onto the top of the branch.

"Don't do anything foolish, son."

It was a little late for that, I thought, struggling with the freaking branch. Twenty feet didn't sound like much, but looking down, I thought the cop was right, I could land funny and die here. "AGH!" I cried, my leg slipping and my body falling away from the branch, my hands overhead holding on with everything I had left.

"Joe!" the cop screamed to another cop. "JOE!"

The fear in his voice scared the hell out of me. He thought I was going to die, I knew he thought I was going to die, he'd seen people die and now he believed he was going to see another one.

Oh, shit, oh, shit, oh, shit.

I wasn't dying, I wasn't going to die, and I flung my leg at the branch and heaved myself over on top of it.

"Good job, son! Good job! Now just hold still. Hold still and we'll come get you."

"No," I said, my entire body limp against the branch, my arms hanging down like noodles on either side.

"It'll be OK, just relax," the old cop coaxed. He was maybe six feet away, his voice calm, gentle, like we were sitting around the kitchen table. "We'll come get you," he said.

"I said no."

"It's going to be OK now."

"You come after me, I'll jump," I said, not moving, still breathing hard, the side of my head still resting on the branch, my hand with the cut throbbing. It wasn't much of a threat, jumping from twenty feet, but clearly the cop didn't want to see me get hurt.

"Son, don't be an idiot."

"I'll come down," I told him. "Just not yet."

"All right, all right, that's fine," the cop said, loudly, like he was reading lines. "You take your time, and when you're ready to come down, we'll help you. I'll go tell my partner what's going on. You just rest."

I wanted some more papaya juice and vodka, was what I wanted. I still felt kind of drunk, but kind of drunk wasn't enough, not when I'd just jumped into a tree to get away from the police.

One of the other cops shined a spotlight up at me, and that's when I realized I didn't have forever, I had no idea if I could trust these guys to leave me alone or not. Would they try storming the tree with a SWAT team? After the stories Robin told us about getting arrested during protest marches, there was no way of knowing what the police would do.

I looked around, the spotlight making the bark look frosty white. Up just above me was a spot where three branches divided from the trunk and made for a good spot to sit. To get there I needed to climb down a little.

"That's it, easy does it," the cop holding the light called, thinking he was coaxing me down as I stretched a foot to the next branch. "Hey, HEY, what are you doing?" he shouted, when I started climbing back up.

The three branches up above were a lot thinner and seemed flimsier than the one that nearly dislocated my shoulder. I held on tight as I scooted my butt into the snug spot between them, and when I finally felt steady, I noticed my left hand hurt like hell, could practically feel the blood oozing out. I pointed my palm down to look at it in the spotlight and saw the whole hand smeared with blood, dark red clots leaking.

"Hi, son," the old cop called.

"How're you doing?"

"What's up, kid?"

It took me a second to realize they thought I was waving. They were down there, waving back, all friendly-like. I pulled some pages out of my pants. I considered ripping them up and tossing them into the wind, but I'd seen on TV what police forensics can do, so I didn't think tearing up the pages would necessarily work.

So I started eating them.

The first page went down no problem, but then my mouth went dry, like I'd been licking stamps, and I knew I wasn't going to be able to eat twenty whole pages. So I used the spotlight to see where the words were on the page, and tore them out and just ate the words. I didn't want to litter, so I stuffed the blank pieces into my back pocket.

"What are you doing up there, son?" the old cop called to me after I ate a few pages.

"I'll be down in a minute," I told him, cursing Zanny for printing everything in the large font. What was she thinking?

The cops—there were four of them standing around at the bottom of the tree—had a little conference.

"That sure as hell better not be illicit drugs you're ingesting," one of them hollered up, "because you sure as hell won't make it down alive."

LSD. That seemed pretty funny to me, that they thought I might be eating sheet after sheet of LSD.

"No," I called, trying to assure them, not wanting them to think I was trying to poison myself up there.

"Then what the hell are you eating?" the same guy asked.

"Words."

I held tighter to the tree, when I heard Zanny somewhere down below, her voice giving me a sense of vertigo. I wrapped my right arm around a branch and used my bloody hand to block the spotlight from shining in my eyes. There she was. I could see her, standing about halfway between the tree and the cop cars, lights still flashing at the curb. It was dark where Zanny was standing, and all I could see was a silhouette, but I knew it was her.

"Who're you?" the old cop called out, walking over in her direction.

I started in on another sheet, chewing faster, knowing she was down there. What if they let her start climbing the freaking tree? It was her tree. Was it legal for them to stop her, even if they wanted to? Plus I could hear her and the old cop talking. They weren't speaking loud enough for me to hear actual words, but I could hear them chatting and it made me nervous.

"What's going on, Officer?" some other guy asked. How many people were down there? If Mrs. Manning brought out chips, they could have a party.

I could see the shape of the new guy as he walked toward the cluster of cops, but I was too busy munching to bother getting a good look at him.

I couldn't believe how filling paper was. Did the ink expand when it got down in your stomach? Was there some kind of chemical reaction? Was it toxic? I was down to the last couple of pages, so it wasn't like I was going to stop now, but I was a little dizzy, like the paper and ink had stirred up the alcohol in my system. I wondered if the government had done studies on this, kids who drank too much and ate paper to get even drunker.

The old cop came back, but the new guy was still out there, standing beside Zanny. A neighbor? An FBI agent? I rolled my eyes. Like the FBI would care about some drunk kid hanging out in a tree.

I felt like singing. I was down to my last sheet. Within seconds all the paper evidence that Kurtz ever existed would be gone, and the cops were apparently fine about waiting it out. As long as I was careful climbing down the damn tree, everything would be fine, and I would get through this pretty much unscathed.

"Life is good," I said, out loud, knowing, as I said it, that that was something Dad said a lot when he'd had a few beers. Life is good. Dad was usually a pretty good drunk—upbeat and personable. What was it that alcohol does, I wondered. Why couldn't people get there, wherever there was, without the alcohol? Didn't alcohol just make you more of yourself? Why was that so good for Dad? Did he spend his life holding himself back?

I was down to half a page when the new guy walked from the shadows toward the cluster of police.

"Ah, there he is," the new guy said. He had asked the old cop what was going on. He was young-looking, in a black sweater with something hanging around his neck. A camera. He had a camera, and he was grabbing hold of it and pointing it up at me as I swallowed the last few words.

Snap.

I blinked, my eyes surprised by the flash.

I had no idea this one photograph would be so funny, so clever, so perfect, so lucky, that it would appear on the cover of three photography magazines, that it would make me and Zanny rich and famous, and that it would make me feel, for the rest of my life, like I would never again fall madly in love.

Sixteen

Love.

It was right there in my hand. If you've seen the photograph, you've seen me holding the word right there in my hand, my hand up by my mouth, my mouth open, ready to eat. Love. I don't know anything about cameras and photography, but apparently it's a miracle the photographer, Harold Smith, was using the perfect telephoto lens and was able to get that kind of detail so that the printed word love is visible right before it goes in my mouth.

Not to mention that Zanny happened to print the e-mails out in a large font so she could tape them on the wall and read them. Not to mention that Harold Smith happened to be driving by that night with a 105 lens on his camera. Not to mention that Harold Smith happened to take the picture as I was about to stuff that particular word in my mouth.

Love.

The photograph's so perfect, some people are convinced we set it up. Even with the four cops all releasing signed statements that they were witnesses, they saw the whole thing, and nothing about it was set up. The cops have even taken lie detector tests, but there are still people out there who think they're all lying.

Or they think Harold Smith somehow tampered with the photograph. Experts have looked at the negative, and they're convinced no one could have done anything to it, but some people out there still aren't convinced, still do not believe any photographer could get that lucky.

In a way, I don't blame them. It's freaky, that I'd be sitting in a tree, eating these love letters, eating my words, as everyone keeps saying, and that one word I'd be holding in my hand would be that one. Love. It really is like a miracle.

A miracle that made people rich. No wonder people are suspicious—Phil Nelson has been able to make two ordinary kids rich and famous from this single photograph of one of them looking like an idiot up in a tree.

What they don't realize is that we're not two ordinary kids. They don't realize that Zanny is anything but ordinary, that Zanny has been waiting for something like this forever, that Zanny has been looking for the perfect story and knew right away this could be it.

If we told it right.

If we didn't blow it.

If I didn't lock myself in a hotel room and try to tell the truth.

Mom and Dad were both at the hospital when we drove up in the police cruiser. I didn't get why the police were taking me to the hospital. I'd gotten down the tree OK, and Harold Smith had gone to his car and had come back with a couple of clean napkins for the cut on my hand. It was throbbing on every heartbeat, but I showed Officer McGuire, the old cop, how the bleeding had mostly stopped. He shook his head and explained that any minor who had been drinking was considered a medical case.

My mom thought that was ridiculous. "Look at him! Talk to him! He's fine! He's sober!"

"Judy," Dad said, softly.

Mom ignored him. She argued with Officer McGuire, then argued with another cop with him, then complained to the emergency room admissions clerk. Dad and I were standing outside this little white cubicle thing, embarrassed, so we didn't hear what the clerk whispered to Mom.

"A psychological consult?" Mom shouted, her voice carrying across the entire emergency room. I could feel Dad look at me, his eyes big.

"What?" he asked.

I didn't even look back at him, and he stepped into the white cubicle with Mom and the police and the clerk. I was all alone and could have made a run for it, but I was sober enough to have some idea of just how bad things were already.

"He what?" Mom asked.

I shut my eyes, just wanted to go to sleep. Mom and Dad came out of the cubicle and I could tell they didn't really believe what the people in the cubicle just told them.

Broke into a house? Jumped out a window? Sat in a tree eating paper?

The three of us had to wait in a curtained-off area for two hours, and Mom was not about to let me just lie down and go to sleep. She didn't even give me any sympathy when this nurse cleaned out the cut in my hand, digging into it with a cotton swab.

"Stop squirming," was all Mom said.

I was actually relieved when I had to talk to the psychiatrist, who had a soft, soothing voice and pointy eyebrows that made him look like Satan. Things were going OK with him until I admitted that I didn't regret what I did. I told him that I definitely would do it all over again—I was so glad those words were gone, that they were at that very minute digesting in my gut, there was no doubt in my mind that I would do it all over again.

Probably not the right thing to admit to a psychiatrist.

He decided I needed to stay overnight for observation. Which was fine with me. I wasn't looking forward to any ride home with Mom and Dad. He even gave me the choice of whether or not to say good-night to them.

"Can you tell them I love them?" I asked. I felt guilty about dragging them through all this, but I could have cried I was so happy I didn't have to see them again that night.

I barely remember a nurse ushering me into a tiny green room with bare walls and a hospital bed. My head landed on the pillow and the next thing I knew, in the morning some guy was waking me up.

"What?" I was so foggy I realized I was in a hospital before I remembered what I was there for. Then it hit me. "Oh, shit."

"Man, you can say that again."

I looked up and saw a man in a green scrubs chuckling to himself and shaking his head as he checked off things on a clipboard.

"What?" I asked him, looking at his name tag. George. Nurse George.

"Just like you said," George told me. "Oh, shit."

"Why? What's going on?"

He wouldn't meet my eyes, just kept smiling. I tried to think back to the night before, wondering if I forgot something. What was so funny? Did I do something funny? Besides the whole tree thing?

George took my temperature and blood pressure and gave me an aspirin and changed the bandage on my hand.

"Good luck, kid," he told me, and laughed again as he left.

I wondered what time it was, wondered if I could still make it to school on time and just kind of disappear into the crowd. I just wanted to get this over with. There would probably be something in the police blotter in the newspaper, but I was a minor, they had to keep my name out of it. Plus they never got too specific. When Brandon Richardson crashed his dad's Porsche and puked all over the cop, all they mentioned in the paper was that there'd been a car accident on Brentwood involving an inebriated minor.

The morning psychiatrist came in. He was younger than the guy with the eyebrows and faster with a diagnosis.

"You don't look crazy to me," he said, grabbing the clipboard George the Nurse had left behind.

I watched him scribble for a while. "Do you know what time it is?" I asked.

"Does anybody really know what time it is?" he said, flipping pages on my chart. "Who would think you would find that kind of philosophical depth in a pop song? Especially one you're too young to have even heard of. It's around seven, I think, but you won't be going anywhere you want to be going for a while, I'm afraid. The police usually conveniently forget about a kid like you they've dropped off in the middle of the night, but after seeing the papers, they came back for you."

"Papers?" Did the Mannings file court documents against me? Were they pressing charges? "What do you mean, papers?"

The psychiatrist hesitated. "No one's been in here to see you?"

"Only the nurse," I said. "He was just here."

"He didn't say anything about what's outside?"

"Why? What's outside?"

Instead of answering, the psychiatrist looked at the floor and bit his lip.

"Are you making this up? Is this some kind of test?"

"You need to remember," he said, looking at me, "that everything passes. It's a good thing to remember anytime, but it's something you're really going to need to keep in mind right now. Time wipes out everything, eventually."

"What—am I going to jail?" I immediately imagined the very worst thing that can happen in jail, the thing that supposedly happens in jail every time a young guy goes to the freaking bathroom.

And just as I was imagining it, the door opened and two cops walked in.

"I'm going to jail?" I asked the psychiatrist, trying to stop the quiver in my voice.

The psychiatrist shook his head.

"No such luck, kid," the tall cop said.

"Would sure make our lives a hell of a lot easier if you were." The short cop sounded resentful, like I'd intentionally ruined his day.

I didn't understand, but I was afraid to ask.

"We good to go, doc?" the tall cop asked.

The psychiatrist nodded. "Mom and Dad already signed off on him."

God, that didn't sound good.

The short cop stepped out in the hallway and motioned me to the left.

"I thought it was this way," I said, pointing to the right, remembering the way out, knowing that was the way out, even looking up at a red exit sign hanging from the ceiling, pointing to the right.

The short cop sighed, like he was tired of all this crap. "We're going this way," he said.

"Into the hospital?" I didn't get what this was about. Didn't the psychiatrist just say I didn't look crazy? Were they going to run more tests? Scan my brain? Why were the cops there?

"We're going to take a side exit," the tall cop said, patting me on the back. "It'll be easier on all of us."

"Why?"

"Because you're a very popular fellow," the short guy said, grabbing me hard by the elbow and pushing me along.

The three of us went down a number of hallways. At one point we came upon two women in blue scrubs who watched me and then burst out laughing once we passed.

"Your fan club," the short cop said. He smelled like the green mouthwash Grandma used to use.

We got to an emergency exit door with a panic bar on it that said an alarm would sound if the door was opened, but the small cop banged it open anyway. I still had only my shirt on, and it was freezing out, but the cop car was right there with the engine running, and the two of them hustled me toward the backseat.

"Hey, over here! He's over here!"

I turned and saw down at the corner of the building some guy running toward us with a camera.

"Shit," the short cop said.

"Just get him in the car."

A bunch of other people came tearing around the corner of the building, most of them with cameras.

"Come on, come on!"

"Watch your head."

As I got pushed into the back seat, I saw a TV camera turn the corner of the building. The short cop almost slammed the door on my leg, and the tall cop had the car moving just as the short cop jumped into the front seat. I looked out the back window and saw the crowd of people slowing down and taking whatever pictures they could get.

"It's like he's goddam Lady What's-Her-Name," the short cop complained.

"Diana," the tall cop said.

I was biting my lip. "Do they think I'm somebody else?" I asked them.

The short cop was opening up a Dunkin Donuts bag, releasing the smell of powdered sugar. "They think you're some goddamn kid who sat up in a tree eating goddamn love letters."

"Are you?" the tall cop asked, looking at me in the rear view mirror.

"Oh, he's the kid, all right," the short cop said, biting into his jelly donut as he tossed the newspaper back at me. On the bottom of the front page was a big blow-up of the picture the guy took the night before when I was sitting up in the tree. Above it was the headline:

Star-Crossed Lover Eats His Words

I stared at the headline, stared back at the picture. It was an incredible picture of me staring at the camera, looking scared, looking goofy, my mouth open, the word love right there in my hand. Oh, my God. I couldn't stand looking at the photograph, but I didn't have enough strength to look away. Oh, my God. I kept realizing different awful things about this, different people who would see it. Dad. Jake. Mom. Zanny.

Everyone. Everyone in my entire universe.

"Oh, shit," I whispered.

"You're famous, kid," the short cop told me, looking through the windshield, sounding almost jealous. "Couple of buddies at work said they were passing around that photograph on the *Today* show. Supposedly it's bound to win some big awards."

"For what it's worth," the tall cop said, looking at me in the rearview mirror, "my wife heard the story and thought you sounded like a great kid."

"Oh, yeah," the short cop said. "You're a big hit with the middle-aged married women. They're going to be all over you. Oooooooo, what a sweeeetieeee."

"Hey, leave him alone," the tall cop said.

"I'm just saying. He could do OK with that divorce group my ex belongs to. Those women are begging for this kind of crap."

What kind of crap? I wanted to ask him. What kind of crap was I? I pressed my fingertips into my forehead as I started to read the article, which said nothing about me and Zanny being friends, so I just sounded like a complete wacko from left field, sending her these anonymous e-mails when I didn't even know her.

"I'll give you ten-to-one he gets some kind of movie deal out of this," the short cop said. "It's like that guy who bought all those frozen foods, remember?"

"How's it like that?"

"You do something stupid, and you end up with a movie deal."

"What are you talking about?" The tall cop was fed up. "The frozen dinner guy never got a movie deal."

The newspaper story continued on B-1, but they didn't give me the B-section, and I sure wasn't going to ask for it.

"Lenny said he got a movie deal," the short cop claimed. "He saw it in the paper."

"What paper? Lenny's an idiot."

I looked up from the paper. We were turning into the parking lot behind the police station. "What—what's going on?" I asked.

"You're busted, kid," the short cop said. "That's what's going on."

"The charges'll be dropped," the other cop said, "but we've got to take you in and get fingerprints and go through the whole rigmarole. Your parents are here. Your lawyer's already arranged bail."

My lawyer? I had a lawyer? I needed bail?

"Oh, Jesus Christ!" the young cop said.

A mob of people was gathered behind the police station. Still cameras, video cameras, at least two television cameras. They all came trotting in our direction.

"I told you," the short cop said. "A goddamn movie deal."

"OK, you grab him," the tall cop said, pulling into a parking spot, "and I'll run interference."

"Hey, take this," the short cop said, holding up a wooden billy club. "It might come in handy."

The tall cop looked at him and shook his head, disgusted. "Let's just get this done, OK?"

I wanted a mask, a pillowcase, some way of hiding myself. I hadn't had a walking-around-in-my-underwear dream in years, but this felt like one.

The short cop climbed out and opened the door and snapped his fingers. "OK, kid. Move. Move. Move. Move."

"OK, FOLKS, YOU'RE GOING TO NEED TO LET US DO OUR JOB HERE!" the tall cop was telling people. "CAN WE GET A LANE HERE? WE NEED A LANE!"

"You wanted to be famous," the short cop said, squeezing my arm hard.

"What?" I asked him. What was he talking about? I didn't want to be famous. I didn't want any of this. I was just trying to protect myself, trying to make sure those words I wrote didn't stick around for people to laugh at. I didn't do anything. Not really. I did one dumb thing, and then a guy took a picture of it, some guy took this bizarre photograph, this amazingly bizarre photograph. It was the photograph, it wasn't me, it was the photograph that ended up on the freaking *Today* show. I just happened to be in the photograph.

And now people were laughing. Even these people with the cameras, they were laughing.

"Hey, Jim."

"Way to go, Jim!"

"How's the stomach feeling, Jimmy?"

That got a laugh, a huge laugh. The tall cop was slowly making way for us, the short cop behind me, holding tight onto my arm and pushing at me. These girls appeared, girls my age, a dozen maybe, holding up pens.

"Can I get your autograph?"

"Please, Jim? Please?"

They were all smiling, laughing. Oh, God.

"Make way, folks," the tall cop hollered. "Make way."

One girl, brown hair, very pretty, got right in my face and held up a pen and pink paper. "How about it, Jim?" she asked, smiling.

"Why are you doing this?"

"Come on! Come on!" the short cop barked.

"Please?" the brown-haired girl asked.

"Is this funny?" I asked her.

Her face changed, the smile gone. I was too embarrassed to look at her.

"You don't get it," I said. "I wasn't trying to be funny."

"Go, go, go. Come on," the short cop screamed in my ear.

"I know," the brown-haired girl said, dropping the pen and pink paper and throwing her arms around my neck and kissing me on the lips, kissing me hard, kissing me for real.

Seventeen

Carly Mansfield. The girl who kissed me behind the police station is Carly Mansfield, and I actually think she deserves a percentage of all the money we've made.

The lawyers sat me and Zanny down early on and told us not to say stuff like that, about people who helped make it all happen, because they don't want to be giving our money away. But the fact is, if Carly Mansfield hadn't kissed me behind the police station, then Mr. Nelson wouldn't have gotten the idea of paying that woman in New York and that woman in Hoboken to kiss me, and the whole kissing thing wouldn't have happened, and he probably never would have thought up the underwear thing. And me and Zanny wouldn't have gotten all this free publicity and wouldn't have appeared on Oprah and *Love Doesn't Grow on Trees* wouldn't have become a best-seller.

And I wouldn't be in this hotel room, drinking from a two-liter bottle of soda, eating chips, knowing there are only two possibilities about Zanny. I've been locked in here for thirty-six hours now, wondering how she could possibly think I was crazy. It just doesn't make sense. I'm normal, pathetically normal. I'm not wacked and Zanny knows I'm not wacked. The problem is, if she knows I'm not wacked, there's only one other possibility.

She's completely betrayed me.

Mr. Halcyon said , "I can handle the legal side."

He and Mom and Dad and I were sitting around the bare table in the empty room at the back of the police station. There were no blinds and the windows were shatterproof glass. I wondered if the police worried about prisoners trying to kill themselves, but then I thought, couldn't you just bash your head against the edge of the table? Wouldn't that be enough, if you swung at it hard enough?

"The legal issues are going to be minimal," Mr. Halcyon claimed, "but you're going to want to get an agent who can negotiate with the Mannings."

Mom leaned forward. "I thought you said they weren't pressing charges."

"No, they're not," Mr. Halcyon admitted. "Although they may change their minds if someone starts talking to them about the financial implications."

I saw Mom and Dad look at each other.

Mr. Halcyon cleared his throat. "They will probably want a piece of the action."

Dad was shaking his head. "What action?"

Mr. Halcyon put his hands flat on the table. "I don't know much about these things," he said, "but I suspect, given the circumstances, that there are significant financial implications."

"What are you talking about?" Mom asked.

"A movie deal," I muttered, miserably.

Mr. Halcyon nodded. "Possibly a movie deal, possibly a book deal. It all depends on how you handle the situation. But you need to understand that the photograph of your son has become an enormous story. My secretary called about twenty minutes ago and said the phone at my office has been ringing off the hook. I suspect if you checked your messages at home, you'd find dozens of agents already trying to contact you."

"I don't understand," Dad said.

"Mr. O'Reilly, people are interested in the story behind the photograph." Mr. Halycon spoke slowly, like he was getting paid by the minute. "Apparently your son wrote love letters—"

"They weren't love letters," I blurted out.

"—and then stole them back and ate them in a tree. Given the remarkable photograph taken by Mr. Smith, people may be willing to pay you significant sums to buy your son's story."

"It's not for sale," I said.

Mr. Halcyon ignored me. "It could turn into quite a marketable story, Mr. and Mrs. O'Reilly. With college bills coming. . . . "

"Jimmy says it's not for sale," Mom told him, patting my knee.

"Mom," I said, pulling my knee away.

"Oh, Jimmy!" she'd hollered, jumping out of her chair when she saw me led through the back door of the police station. She hugged me saying Jimmy, Jimmy, Jimmy, but she was crying so I couldn't say anything. Now not only was she calling me Jimmy, but she had to pat my freaking knee.

"No need to make a rash decision," Mr. Halcyon said, standing up before I could say anything. Like go to hell.

A cop ushered me and Mr. Halcyon downstairs while somebody finished the paperwork. There were three small cells for youth offenders down there with real bars, just like you see in prison movies. She unlocked the last cell and left the door open and walked away. Mr. Halcyon sat down on the little bench inside. He was wearing a dark suit and reminded me of the undertaker at Grandma's funeral, the one Dad said had perfected the smile of sorrow.

The female cop came back with the papers and handed them to Mr. Halcyon. He put them down on the bench and said all I had to do was sign, take the pink copy, and go. I could get out of there, I was free, all I had to do was sign my name.

I stood there, holding onto the bars, staring at the papers.

"There's no hitch, nothing tricky," Mr. Halcyon said, pointing down at the papers on the bench. "You're just saying you won't break the law, and you'll come back for your court date." He'd already signed, over on the right, a big loop in the R in Robert. How'd he know I wasn't going to break the law?

"I just. . . " I shook my head. I had absolutely no reason not to sign, nothing to explain my hesitation. I stared down at the thin sheets of paper so I wouldn't have to look at Mr. Halcyon.

"Take your time," he said, waving his hand impatiently, his voice tight. "I'll be upstairs with your mom and dad. Waiting."

The door to the cell was wide open. Mr. Halcyon went down the hall and muttered something to the cop.

I didn't take my eyes off the papers. I needed to sign, I knew I was going to need to sign. Mom was going to be down in like three seconds wanting to know what the problem was, and Dad would be adding up Mr. Halcyon's hourly rate like we'd left a cab outside with the meter running. I knew I should just sign the damn paper.

But where the hell was I going to go?

Home? Was I going to go home? And sit at the kitchen table with Dad staring at me and Robin cooking some sort of arugula stew for lunch? What about Mom? She'd want to be there, too, she'd want to talk about it, Mom was a huge believer in talking, as if talking could make things disappear. And they weren't going to disappear. People weren't going to let them disappear.

I didn't want to sign because I didn't want to get out of there. I didn't want to face the marketable story. Jail was better than facing that. The cell in the basement was like a campfire in the woods where I could be alone, and I knew any place else was going to involve people and cameras and decisions and mistakes and ramifications and none of it was going to be as simple as this right now. I reached up and gently touched my lips with my fingertips. Even that kiss. That kiss behind the police station had been so simple. I'd never been kissed like that. It was so complete, so absolute, no one had ever wanted to kiss me so much, had ever pressed her lips against mine like that. I knew I was crazy to even think about it because the girl was some nut who didn't even know me and probably went around attacking rock stars, but just the way she looked at me, and then the way she held onto me so completely, it felt simple and pure.

"Hey."

I turned. Zanny was outside the cell, her hands clutching the bars. "Oh, God," I said. "No, no. no. Who—? Who let you—? No. Just—oh, God, I cannot believe this."

"Will you calm down?" Zanny asked, walking through the open door.

I stood up and backed away like she was contagious. "Zanny—"

"I just want your autograph."

I walked into a corner and grabbed the bars. "Please. Just—"

"Jim—what is wrong with you?"

"Nothing. Nothing. Could you just—go away?"

"You are such an idiot."

"OK. You're right. That's fine. Now could you go away?"

"Jim. This could very well be our last chance to talk for days."

"That's OK," I said. "That's—days is fine. Weeks. Months. Years."

"You don't have to sound so happy about it."

I was still holding onto the bars, still facing the corner. "Zanny, there just isn't much to say here."

"Are you kidding me? Tell me you're kidding." Out of the corner of my eye I could see Zanny sit on my bench. "Jim, we have to have a whole plan in place."

I squinted but didn't turn toward her. "What—plan?"

"Didn't your lawyer talk to you about what's going on out there?" Zanny sounded amused, like she was dealing with some little kid who just didn't get it. "You're famous, Jimmy. A celebrity."

"All right," I said.

"That photograph is everywhere. People are talking about you all over America."

"All right."

"Three hundred newspapers picked up the picture of you in the tree."

"Will you stop?" I asked, turning around.

Zanny rolled her eyes. "Oh, come on. You're not going to tell me there isn't a part of you that's loving this, loving every second of it."

I stared at her, shaking my head, dismayed. "Don't you see what this looks like? I'm sitting there, up in a tree. . . "

"Eating your words," Zanny said. "It's perfect. It's brilliant."

"It's idiotic. It's humiliating!"

"Oh, yeah?" Zanny stood up. "That girl who kissed you this morning didn't seem to think so."

I screwed up my face. "Who—how did you find out about that?"

"Oh, come on! You didn't see the cameras in your face?"

"I didn't know they'd take pictures of that."

"Carly Mansfield," Zanny said. "Now she's famous, too."

"What are you talking about? She's a wacko."

"You didn't kiss her like she's a wacko."

"What? Kiss her? I didn't kiss her."

"You sure weren't fighting her off."

I turned around and grabbed the bars again. "I don't believe this."

"Look, it doesn't matter," Zanny said, an edge to her voice. "The point is, America thinks it's cute."

"Cute? What are you talking about, cute?"

"They like you," Zanny said. "Women are absolutely crazy about you."

I remembered what the short cop said in the cruiser: middle-aged women. Women my mother's age. I leaned my head against the bars.

"Don't you see how much fun we can have?"

That turned me around again. "What?" I stared at Zanny. She was smiling, but she seemed like a different person. "Are you trying to get back at me?"

Zanny walked toward me, smiling. "Look, silly, you know who I just spent the last half hour talking to?"

"Zanny—I don't care."

"Phil—Nelson," she said. She sounded like she was reading scripture, saying the name.

"Who's Phil Nelson?"

"Oh, my God! Jimmy!" Zanny stomped away but then stomped right back and stood in front of me. "How could you not know Phil Nelson?"

I pointed past her to the papers still sitting there on the bench for me to sign. Suddenly getting out of there seemed a whole lot more appealing. "Could you move, please?"

"My nine-year-old niece knows Phil Nelson," Zanny said. "Nothing happens without Phil Nelson. *The Millennium Marriage? The Rat Race?* Even that movie about those awful people! None of it ever would have happened without Phil Nelson."

I tried to move around her, but Zanny blocked my way. "Look," I told her. "I need to go sign that piece of paper so I can get out of here."

"Jim," Zanny said, grabbing my shoulders.

I needed CPR, my eyes all over the place, desperate to get away, but not knocking Zanny's hands off my shoulders.

"He wants us to go on Leno," she said.

I was still reacting to the hands on my shoulders, I didn't get a chance to absorb Leno. I'd heard what she'd said, but I couldn't react, I was too busy feeling Zanny's fingers hold me in place. "Could you let go, please?" I asked, barely getting the words out.

"Not until you look at me." Zanny's voice was softer. At all costs, as if she were Medusa ready to turn me into stone, I needed to avoid looking at her. "Just look at me for a second," she said.

"That's—not going to happen," I told her.

"Just for a second, Jim. Just look at me."

"I don't want to look at you."

That's when the lips happened. Zanny's lips on mine. She kissed me, on the lips, slightly parted. Our lips were touching—at least until I pulled away.

"What—this—I—"

"I want to be with you, Jim."

I still couldn't look at her. "Zanny, this isn't—this isn't—" And it wasn't, I could just tell it wasn't what it seemed to be, what it was supposed to be, there was something too easy, too simple.

"Mr. Kurtz," Zanny whispered. "Come with me."

I was breathless, my eyes averted. "Look. You have your story. The story you always wanted. This is your story."

"This is our story."

I was up against the bars, my head turned to one side. Zanny grabbed hold of my chin and turned me toward her.

"We both want this," she said.

And I knew she wasn't lying. We both might have wanted it, but it meant completely different things. Yes, she wanted to be with me, yes, I believed that, but there was nothing stupid, nothing idiotic about what Zanny wanted. Her lips, her kiss was what I'd wanted for months, for years, maybe, without realizing it, but it was nothing like the kiss from the wacko girl outside. Zanny's kiss was real and it was honest, but it wasn't idiotic, it wasn't unselfish or giving, it wasn't something that pulled at you in ways you didn't understand.

"We could spend the summer touring together," Zanny said, grabbing me by the front of my shirt and smiling.

I started shaking my head. "Touring what?"

"A book tour. Phil wants us to do a tour."

"Phil?"

"Phil Nelson. He said to call him Phil."

"Oh, my God."

"He says a book tour is absolutely necessary to maintain momentum."

"But—" I looked around. "What book? There's no book."

Zanny nodded. "I'm already working on it. I'm going to take a couple of weeks off from school."

"You're going to write a book in two weeks?"

"Jim, relax! It's not an issue. Whatever needs to be taken care of can be taken care of. He said all we have to do is show up."

"But—" I tried to breathe. Zanny had let go of my shirt but had left her hands flat on my chest. I needed to get away from the warmth of her palms. "Hold on a second." I turned and grabbed hold of a bar for support, like I'd had too much to drink.

"It'll be a blast," Zanny said.

I swallowed, looking through the bars at a steel door on the other side. The whole summer with Zanny. Traveling around the country with Suzannah Manning. Airports, bookstores, radio stations. Hotel rooms. She'd just finished kissing me, anything could happen. I stared at the door and tried to remember the feel of her lips, tried to remember the moment, but it had happened so fast.

"Best friends since preschool?" Zanny said, behind me. "Getting together junior year in high school? People will love us."

"We both want this."

Those were the words, her words. And we did. We both did. We both wanted this. Not the same way, not for the same reason, but we both wanted it.

"Agh," I said, softly, like I felt a sharp pain somewhere deep inside.

I stared at the steel door, knowing I'd already made the decision, but without any confidence that it was the right decision. It was the only choice I could see, though, the only choice I could believe, the only choice that could get me out of that cell.

"Come on, Jimmy," Zanny whispered.

I held my breath. "OK," I said.

Epilogue

Not exactly as romantic as Zanny made it sound like in *Love Doesn't Grow on Trees,* where we looked into each other's eyes

"with a burning fire of passion joining us together"

Uh—no. I don't remember any passion joining us together.

Don't get me wrong. I was still in love with Zanny Manning. I was embarrassed about the words and the tree and the photograph, but nothing had changed, I still loved her completely, absolutely, stupidly, and I was ready to travel the world with her, no matter what happened, I was willing to take my chances—follow her to the ends of the earth, the whole bit. Then.

And the scary thing is, maybe now I still would. It isn't like everything's different, like someone hit a light switch and I've been able to shake myself free. Zanny might be in some hotel room, crying her eyes out because I'm a nutcase. Or she and Phil Nelson might be at some gala event, drinking champagne and laughing at how they've made America think I'm wacked.

I think I know what Zanny's doing, I have a good guess, but I don't know for sure what's going on out there. It's midnight—except for a couple of ship lights in the harbor, the ocean out there is a vast field of black. All I know about is what's going on in here. And in here, the fact is this:

I don't think I'm over Zanny Manning.

Maybe I am. I can sort of imagine being over Zanny. I mean, Dad was stupid in love with Mom, and eventually he got over it. I don't know how it works exactly, if love wears down or burns out or just gets old and tired, but I can picture a time when I don't think about Zanny every hour of every day.

I realize this is not the way things were supposed to happen. America wanted to believe we were this cute, young, happy couple that was going to last forever, just the way it's supposed to happen, but now I don't think that's how it ever works. I think things just work out the way they do, and we're doing OK if we're not jerks and we don't make things worse. There are a lot of people out there who are dying to believe in the way it's supposed to be, and there may be some guy out there who really and truly believes in the way it's supposed to be, but, personally, I think he's the real idiot.

No, this isn't the love story it's supposed to be. But nutcase or not, I'm about to walk out of this hotel room and give my mom and dad (back together just for this trip to California) a hug and wave to the cameras and smile like I haven't smiled in months because it's my smile again, it's me. It feels good. Here I am. Me.

I may even give Carly Mansfield a call. She may be a wacko, she may not even talk to me now that I've totally screwed up being rich and famous, but that kiss behind the police station felt real, felt absolute, felt beyond where most people are willing to go.

Sorry, America.

The End

Colin Neenan grew up in New York City and has always lived in the East. He's been a doorman, a chauffeur and a census worker, but now he's a librarian in a middle school, where he shouts at kids and occasionally scares the sixth graders.

He's been writing forever and hopes that after you finish this book, you'll read his two other books, *In Your Dreams* and *Live a Little*. His daughters claim he eats too much salsa and sings too loud; they also call themselves modern Cinderellas because he makes them empty the dishwasher. The three of them live in Connecticut and can be reached at *neenancolin@hotmail.com*.